TIGHT LIKE THAT

Books by Jim Christy

TIGHT LIKE THAT

< stories >

Jim Christy

ANVIL PRESS | VANCOUVER | 2003

Anvil Press
6 West 17th Avenue (rear)
Vancouver, B.C. V5Y 1Z4   CANADA
www.anvilpress.com

NATIONAL LIBRARY OF CANADA CATALOGUING IN PUBLICATION DATA

Christy, Jim, 1945-
Tight like that: stories / Jim Christy.

ISBN 1-895636-49-3

I. Title.
PS8563.I4763K58 2003   C813'.54   C2003-910130-4
PR9199.3.C4983T53 2003

Printed and bound in Canada
Cover and book design: HeimatHouse

Represented in Canada by the Literary Press Group
Distributed by the University of Toronto Press

The publisher gratefully acknowledges the financial assistance of the B.C. Arts Council, the Canada Council for the Arts, and the Book Publishing Industry Development Program (BPIDP) for their support of our publishing program.

You wearing those dresses
Sun comes shining through
Can't believe my eyes
All that mess belongs to you

— BIG JOE TURNER

CONTENTS

MEXICAN
STAND-OFF

Midnight, Imogene got off the elevator, crossed the lobby of the Sandman Inn aware of people checking her out, of tongues clucking, eyes rolling. So Imogene gave her hips an extra roll, did a modified bump and grind. Big, nearly six feet tall, wearing the clingy blue sheath number, Imogene liked to think of herself as naturally attractive. No cosmetic surgery freak. One lady, hairdo like she had a lap dog on her head, turned down the corners of her mouth in disgust. Yeah, old bitch, Imogene thought, don't see anything like me where you live which is probably some bible burg like Abbotsford. She'd been there once or, rather, stopped there the one time. A suit and tie picked her up outside the Marble Arch, drove her all the way out the Valley to some motel. Did his business then kicked her out. He must have felt ashamed of himself. Four in the morning, shit. Hey, pal. It's not my fault you had the urge. Just by the front door, guy coming out of the sports bar, gave her a whistle.

9

She looked over, looked him up and down. He said something obscene. Imogene decided he wasn't a spender, just a talker, a time-waster.

She hit the street. Lit up, blew smoke into the air, ignoring young dudes shouting from a car. She considered walking back to familiar surroundings, but her heels were four inches high and she was tired. It had been a busy night. Imogene wanted to call it quits after another trick. Maybe she'd score an all-nighter with an old man. But not too old. The difference was the former did it once and fell asleep; the latter usually couldn't do it and kept her up all night trying. Whatever, she needed a room for the night.

Cab driver was some kind of East Indian. Took her to the Cactus Lounge.

"Pretty lady, you don't have to pay you don't want. You know what I mean?"

"Yeah, I know what you mean, but for five dollars and sixty-five cents you don't even get a pat on the knee."

She paid, got out, and the guy peeled rubber.

Cactus Lounge. Fake desert plants. A wall mural that was supposed to represent Arizona. The joint inspired witticisms. You went in there, scoped the place like she was doing, and the people—you figured they were thinking about partying or making a score or meeting the man with the goods but, no—what most of them were thinking was a new smart-ass comment to make about the Cactus. It usually had something to do with cowpokes or dry land flora and their attributes. The Cactus? It's where the cowpokers hang out. Or, My aren't they a prickly pair. Or, the one she liked best—what the Closet Queen said about a certain dyke duo: Check out that prick-less pair.

10

She went up to the bar, ordered a brandy and milk, wondered which table held out the best possibilities. Jesus, she thought, what a collection. Looks like they let half of maximum security out on a night pass. Them and a couple dozen who looked like they were waiting to take their place. You got your addicts, boosters, molesters, cross-dressers, and some who were all four at once. Yeah, it ain't no good life but it sure as shit is my life. There were even a few normal-looking people in suits. Them's the ones a girl's got to watch out for, Imogene told herself.

And here come Dromboski and Cherry Cherry. Drombo used to play for the Lions until he veered off the straight and narrow, eventually becoming Cherry Cherry's body-guard. And if ever a bitch needed a bodyguard, she was the one. She wasn't the best-looking woman to ever make the scene but, well, it could honestly be said, and Cherry Cherry wasn't loath to say it herself, "I'm twice the woman any of the rest of them are."

They asked each other what was happening. Cherry Cherry had worked a speciality the night before that paid her very handsomely so her and Drombo were just hang-ing out. Imogene inquired as to what was likely.

"Might be potential for you at table seventeen," Cherry Cherry said.

There was an acrylic painting of a rattlesnake uncoiling on red desert soil, ready to strike the young man at table seventeen on the back of his tousle-haired head. Looked like a career student who'd had a long career. He had a draft beer and a spiral notebook in front of him.

"Christ," Imogene said, "when's the last time you saw anybody wearing a button-down shirt?"

11

"Guy's with the paper," Drombo said in his curious high voice. "Says he's doing features on how people live down here in what he calls 'the tenderloin.' Used to hate reporters when I was with the team. Questions they ask. Why, one time . . ."

"You talk to him a coupla minutes," Cherry Cherry said, "he'll give you a few bucks. He's between interviews now."

"I'll get more than a few bucks off of him."

Imogene finished her brandy and milk and started over. Should have been some Billy Rose behind her. She used to use that in her act back when she had an act. More money to be made in her current occupation.

The fellow looked up from his scribbling when she was two steps away. Imogene saw him appraising her, paying special attention to the part below the waist, the sheath creasing in a wide V, then getting flustered, swallowing, adjusting his glasses with clean, rather small fingers.

Imogene sat right down, fastened her eyes on him, gave him the fetching little simper, said, "Well, start firing, handsome."

He hemmed and hawed, and finally asked her what she did.

"Whatever you want me to do, sugar."

Then he didn't so much hem and haw as stammer and stutter. "Uh, no, I mean . . ."

"Yeah I know what you mean. I'm a working girl, you know, as in prostitute."

And he got into it again, Imogene wondering how'd he make it in his chosen profession with that kind of interviewing technique. "Look, sugar, I see you're a little nervous being down here on the seamy side."

12

"No, no, it's . . ."

"It's me? Oh, you're so sweet, sugar. Hey, let me order you a Cactus Special. One of those and you'll be the glib smooth interviewer you usually are. Tequila, vodka, lime and grenadine. Two of them and you'll be asking my price."

"No, I . . ."

She called the cocktail waitress, ordered a Cactus Special for the fellow, Lorne, and another brandy and milk for herself. The drinks arrived, they and Imogene putting him at ease. Hey, it was her job. She had to tell him all about her childhood, having to do her uncle—her mother's brother—Imogene sure her mother knew it was happening. Her parents splitting up. The foster homes. The high school drugs. The adult drugs. Alleys and dives. The attempts at show biz and then the street.

He had some wispy hairs above his upper lip which he probably convinced himself was a dashing moustache. He asked predictable questions, like "Wouldn't you like to get out of The Life?"—trying to make her think he was familiar with the term, The Life, but over-emphasizing it—"and find a decent respectable job?"

Her telling him no, saying, "Look, enough about me. What about you?"

He was a year-and-a-half out of journalism school. Had worked a year of that with his hometown paper up north somewhere before grabbing a spot with a big city daily.

"I'll be doing a six-part series on conditions down here. Getting material from the inside."

"The inside?"

"Yes, really getting the lives of users and hookers, criminals and down-and-outs. The real stories."

13

He had smooth cheeks and an unlined forehead, tiny little pink zit above the left eye halfway to his hairline, and a button nose. So young, Imogene thought, so innocent. But the lad's innocence was tinged with arrogance. Hell, maybe it was his protective armour. I mean it takes a lot of guts to come around here asking questions if you're so completely straight.

"You think you're getting real stories, telling everybody you're a reporter and writing it all down while they're talking to you? Pardon me, handsome, but you got your head down there taking notes and missing most of what's going on."

"How else should I go about it?"

Him asking it, pretending to want her advice but not keeping the condescension entirely out of his voice.

"You have to live down here. Go to one of the hotels, get a room and leave your notebook in it. Make the streets, live the life. Remember what you heard. Write it down later. Hey, looks like you're ready for another one."

"Oh, I shouldn't . . ."

"Sure you should. You got to start somewhere."

The drinks came. They touched glasses.

"You got to be ready for anything that happens, Mr. Reporter. Got to open yourself up to stuff." Imogene winked. "You know what I mean?"

"Uh . . ."

"But at the same time you got to be wary of everybody." She laughed. "And that includes me."

Cherry Cherry walked by the table, nodded to them. Imogene saw Lorne following her with big eyes that hadn't seen much his whole life.

14

Imogene reached under the table, put a hand on his knee, got his attention back where it belonged.

"Forget about her, sugar. I got what you need right here."

"You do?"

"Yeah."

Imogene reached further until her ear was on the table and her index fingernail flicking at his fly. Nice bulge down there, Imogene thought. Lorne gave a nervous look around.

"Hey, you got nothing to worry about in here, believe me. This bunch has seen everything. A donkey show in the corner wouldn't raise an eyebrow."

Lorne didn't seem to object to her fingertip explorations so Imogene suggested they go somewhere private. He stood. "Mmmm," she said, "I like a man so quickly erect."

The guy actually blushed. Walking to the door, she gave his rear end a squeeze and looked to the tables, winked, playing to the audience. Lorne was oblivious.

Out on Hastings, the folks were staggering and swearing or lying on the sidewalks. One guy was looking in a store window and cursing. He must have seriously disliked the guy staring back at him because he threw a round-house right over the steel bars and shattered the window. Then he stood there, bleeding hand hanging down. "Where'd you go, you fuckin' dink?" he cried.

Five minutes later, they were in the alley between Hastings and Pender, stepping over two passed-out kids in a doorway by a dumpster. Lorne observed them closely, saw the transparent plastic tube tied around the upper arm of one of them, and reached for his notebook. "Don't take that out around here, sugar," Imogene said. "Remember it, write it later. Come on."

They went through a door. Just inside was a big, bald, hairy man wearing only boots and a leather jockstrap. He looked at Lorne. Looked at Imogene. "You vouch for your partner?"

"Yeah."

The guy opened the other door.

Imogene went in first, took three steps, looked over her shoulder and saw the reporter had already turned back to the exit. She grabbed his arm, turned him around. "Look, I'll only be a minute," she screamed over the pounding music. "I'll get us a bottle. Gimme twenty bucks and wait here. Against the wall."

Imogene disappeared into the crowd and it was four and a half minutes before she returned. Lorne had his back against the wall and the spiral notebook in front of his crotch. "Sugar, you really shouldn't have been taking notes in here."

"I wasn't."

"Oh, I get it. Self-protection."

Out in the alley, she asked him what he thought of it in there.

"Well, it's, uh, not my scene." Not wanting to come right out and tell her it was disgusting and he felt sick.

"You look a little green under the gills," She wrapped her arm in his. She was at least four inches taller. "A little of this brandy and even more of me ought to cure what ails you."

They got back to Hastings and Imogene led him across the street to the Mexico Hotel.

"How 'bout this?"

"Fine," he said. "I was thinking of doing a piece on skid row hotels."

16

Imogene thinking Christ, the Mexico is upscale for around here but saying, "Yeah, well this is a good place to start."

Before Imogene could react, Lorne brought out his VISA, laid it on the counter. The clerk looked like Rod Steiger. He glanced at it like it was a card from a deaf and dumb guy who could stay deaf and dumb and hungry and homeless for all she cared.

"You gotta pay cash here, sugar," Imogene said.

They had to climb three flights of stairs, Imogene going first, letting him check out the goods.

Inside, she poured both of them some brandy.

"Bottoms up," she said coyly, but it didn't register. Imogene wondered what they taught in journalism school.

The way the kid went at his drink, it reminded Imogene of a chicken pecking, the brandy too strong for big drinks, and him too nervous to drink slowly. She started talking dirty to him and he seemed to like it. She made two more drinks, brought his over, started unbuttoning his shirt. Imogene bent down to kiss his chest. It was hairless. She thought she could feel him trembling. Well, get ready to tremble some more she said to herself and started to go down on her knees, seeing, on her descent, the red neon hotel sign out the window: MEXICO.

Just as she got her hand on his belt buckle, the kid stepped back. Imogene stood, "Whatever you want, honey."

Lorne looked over at the bed.

"You want me there?"

He nodded.

"Want to undress me?"

He shook his head.

17

"Cat got your tongue?"

He nodded again.

"Relax, have another sip of brandy. I'll do whatever you want. I'm your sex slave."

Lorne pecked his brandy, licked his lips.

"Uh, well, if you just lay back . . . "

Imogene lay back on the bed and Lorne came over, climbed up on the bed at the foot, started running his hands up her legs, pushing her skirt up. The kid was breathing heavy. Imogene wondered what was going to happen next. Lorne began working with his tongue above where the stockings ended, worked his way up. Imogene holding her breath. He's almost there.

Then an "Oohhh!" like a cry of pain, and the kid backed up so fast he almost fell off the bed.

"Hey, listen. I did warn you, remember. Don't trust anybody down here, not even me."

Then Imogene thought, Shit, don't let him get out of here with the money.

But, no, the kid didn't get off the bed, just sat back on his haunches looking devastated, like he was watching the old family home go up in flames. But what he was watching was between Imogene's legs. Imogene sighed, reached under and untied the thin satin cord.

"Well now that you know, I might as well release these things. It's not easy wandering around for hours like this. But listen, don't feel disgusted, eh? Or at least try not to show it and make me feel bad. Another thing—you might as well try and get over the shock and get your money's worth. See . . ."

Imogene trying to keep talking so he wouldn't do any-

18

thing nasty. Some of them would flip out, start throwing things around the room, or kicking things, mostly her.

"See, if you thought I was a girl—and you did, didn't you?"

"Yes."

There was actually a little tear in his eye.

"And I kept up the illusion and you had sex with me, then it wouldn't mean you were gay, right?"

Imogene really trying to convince him, thinking this is no fat sweaty creep but a cute young man. What the hell.

But now it was as if the one tear Imogene saw had expanded along his bottom eyelid and the process had begun in Lorne's other eye. He sniffed.

"But," he said. "But . . ."

He sniffed again.

"But what?"

"I *am* gay."

Imogene stared at him.

"Huh?"

Lorne nodded.

"But if you're gay and you thought I was really a girl, why'd . . . ? And if you're gay why don't we, uh, you know?"

Lorne unzipped and Imogene saw the jockstrap, the cup in the pouch.

"Okay, so far so good," Imogene said.

Lorne reached into the pouch and took out a ball of rolled up white socks.

"Real name, Lorna."

"No shit?"

"Yes. I've been passing for a year and a half. Taking my hormones, lifting weights."

Imogene reached down to get the brandy bottle off the floor. Saw the damned sign still glowing red outside the window. She poured them both a generous drink. Said, "Shit, I really wanted to end the night with a good fuck."

"Me too," Lorna said. "I—I've never done it before. I've been too scared. I saw you and I was really . . ."

"Really turned on?"

"Yes."

"Well ain't that a son-of-a-bitch."

"It's four in the morning, I guess I better be going."

"Not out on those streets, sugar. We both might as well sleep here."

Lorna started to say something and Imogene cut her off. "Hey, neither of us have anything to worry about. I mean, there won't be any hanky-panky going on."

"I guess not."

"Yeah, seems what we got here is a Mexican stand-off."

WOMAN IN A LIGHTWEIGHT DRESS

When he awoke and opened his eyes, he was looking at faded roses against a dull grey background, columns of roses separated by sallow borders. His first thought was that the roses were the colour of a car that had been red once upon a time, when the original buyer saw it in the showroom, just the first in a long line of owners who never washed it and who all lived by the sea. Then he thought about being by the sea in someone else's home. He was always on the sea or by the sea.

He was in Honolulu on a cot in the two-room apartment of an old dude called Warren. He turned over and saw a female leg sticking out from under a sleeping bag on the floor. It was a nice white leg or, rather, the tanned leg of a white woman. There were two people under the sleeping bag. The other was Lester Griffins, the black guy he'd met in San Francisco. They'd signed on the ship together.

He was just starting to feel deprived when he recalled he'd had his own girl the night before. Made love with her right on this cot, nobody else paying them any attention in the general rowdiness of the evening. The bottles piling up, blues and old standards on the radio. You could still get that kind of music on the radio back then, 1962. He was forty years old. He'd been working on boats and ships since he was a teenager but he'd never shipped to the Islands before. He'd always wanted to come to Hawaii. It was the last locale he'd had for his mother.

Twenty-one years old, going back to Lewes to visit his father. The old man saying, "I heard somebody saw your mother in Hawaii."

That was it. Didn't say how he'd come across this piece of information, or who was supposed to have seen her or when this had taken place.

He saw the calendar move on the door on the far wall, the door open and Warren appear. Must have been sixty-five years old, Warren, but still a strong-featured, good-looking man even though he was bleary-eyed, needed a shave, grey hair all messed. Or maybe it was more like you looked at him and saw the memory of a strong-featured, good-looking man.

Warren nodded, "I'll put on some coffee and go down the hall to piss."

The woman woke when she heard pots and pans rattling in the kitchen alcove. Sat up, said something like "Uhmmm," noticed one of her breasts was exposed and covered it, with no particular haste, with a corner of the green sleeping bag.

She had a lot of black hair. Thin shoulders. A bony face

and big brown eyes. He liked her looks. She saw him looking at her and smiled. Warren went out into the hall and no sooner was the door closed than she stood up, long slim legs, no fat on her, thick black hair down there too, and she was on the cot with him in three strides. Got under the covers and kissed him. Her breath smelling like sleep and cigarettes. "I like it best in the morning. You want to?"

"Yes, I do."

She turned on her side, offered him her back.

"Okay, sweetie. Give it to me. Uh, the regular place."

He slipped easily inside her. She was sopping wet. She pushed her bony rear end into him and started moving. They found a groove and worked it. Didn't break it when Warren came back into the room. They were almost completely covered by the sheet. He felt like they were kids playing under the covers. She came before he did, her long groan causing him to finish.

"Hey, baby! What's going on?"

Lester was awake.

"I'm not your property," she said. He remembered her name was Hedy.

Lester made no reply.

He turned his head, Lester caught his eye, sort of shrugged.

Hedy whispered in his ear, "His is bigger, he's, uh, you know, but it didn't get me over the edge. I just wanted to try a coloured guy."

"You never tried a coloured guy before?"

She looked in his eyes. "Uh, well, maybe once or twice. Twice, actually."

"Breakfast in bed." Warren was there, holding a tin tray before him, the kind of tray that fastens to collapsible legs so you can eat your dinner in front of the television set. But Warren didn't have a television set. "Only breakfast is only coffee."

Warren brought the tray to them first.

"Milk, Madame? Sugar?"

When it was Lester's turn, he said, "Bet you never served no darkie before."

"Oh, are you a darkie?" Warren came back at him. "I didn't notice."

Lester snorting at that. His dark brown skin, that nose, pomaded hair. No mixed blood there.

Warren set the tray on an enameled kitchen table, drew back dirty curtains. There was a view of rooftops and a sliver of blue water beyond. He asked them when they had to catch their ship.

"Couple days," Lester told him. "What time is it?"

"Quarter to one. P.M."

"Shit," Lester said.

"You late?" Warren said. "You got a date?"

"Yeah, that's it," Lester answered, looked over to Hedy.

Hedy squeezed his thigh under the cover. They were sitting up, backs against the wall. Then she brought her hand out to catch the blanket, stop its slide before it revealed too much.

"Who was that guy I had to throw out before he heaved on the carpet?" Warren asked. "He one of your crew?"

"Never saw him before," he said. "I thought he was a friend of yours."

24

They talked over the night before. A big drinking bout that had started at the Sandwich Islander, moved to a few more dives before winding up back at Warren's place at two in the morning when the night was just getting started.

Half an hour later, Lester said he really had to go. Couldn't keep the lady waiting.

A couple of minutes after that, Warren, watching them, bit his lower lip, muttered, "Think I'll run down to the store, get some bread for toast. Be back in twenty minutes."

Hedy started to giggle. Warren laughed and winked on his way out. They made love again, this time with Hedy on her back. She was good at it. In that position she moved her thing like it was an independent creature.

They finished and got dressed, sat back on the cot, Hedy asking him where his folks were. "My father's in Delaware. Chesapeake Bay area."

"What about your mother?"

"Haven't seen her since I was thirteen."

"What happened to her?"

"Don't know. She just ran off. What about yours?"

"Divorced. My mother lives in Medford, Oregon. My old man remarried. He's somewhere in Florida."

Warren made another pot and some toast. It was a pleasant time, sitting around shooting the breeze. He and Warren not cutting up jackpots, considerate of Hedy. They talked some more about the port, the bars where you were liable to run into guys from ships, how to avoid the military, the Navy sailors.

"All that talk, you guys reminded me I have my own job to go to." Hedy made ready to leave. She worked four-thirty to closing in some joint. He couldn't remember it, even when

25

she said the name. It had been quite a night. They kissed and promised to meet later.

He didn't follow her out. There was still coffee in the pot and Warren had gotten him thinking. So he asked Warren about Honolulu.

"I've been shipping out of here, drifting back here since before the big war. You should have seen this town then."

He talked about some of the characters. Some of the ships.

"I've been at sea most of my life. The only time I've been on land since I was a kid was two years here in the late Forties. Worked on the docks."

"Thought you'd give the beach a try?"

"No, I fell for a dame."

"That'll do it."

"Damn right. It'll do it and do you too."

"What happened? You don't mind my asking."

"Just up and left. Stuffed some clothes in her suitcase said 'I'm sorry, Warren.' And that's all she wrote. She was a fine-looking woman."

Warren rose from the table.

"Come here. Let me show you."

He followed Warren into his bedroom. There were dozens of photographs on the wall, all around the oval mirror that sat on the old-fashioned dresser. Glancing quickly, he saw mostly men and boats, men on the decks of boats, men outside of bars, two men standing at the international date line, two signs pointing in opposite directions, one painted 'Yesterday,' the other, 'Today.'

"No, here," Warren said. "Look at this one first."

He looked, a black and white photograph of a woman in

26

a lightweight dress, white shoes, wind ruffling her hair. She was standing on a wharf, a bollard to her left, ships in the background.

"Jesus," he muttered.

"Yeah," Warren said, not looking at him. "Nice looking, wasn't she?"

He just stared at the photograph of his mother.

"Theresa," Warren said. "That was her name."

"Yeah," he heard himself reply.

Warren talked about her, how great she was.

"Where did she come from?" he asked.

"Funny you should ask. I asked her that once—I mean, it's a natural thing to ask, right?"

"Yeah."

"And she said, 'Here and there. It doesn't matter.' She obviously didn't want to talk about her background, so I never pressed it."

Warren stared at the photograph, looked away.

"Now these pictures here. They're taken all over the world."

He couldn't see the other photographs. He could only see the one.

"I have to go, Warren."

"But . . ."

"Maybe I'll see you later."

He walked out of the room and the apartment, down the dark stairs, out into the bright, busy street. The sidewalks were crowded—he knew they were—and people were talking, cars rolling by. All he could think of was his mother with Warren, up there in that same apartment. Coming down into the street, walking to the corner that he could see through his watering eyes. She never even wrote him a letter, sent a birthday greeting, a goddamned Christmas card. Could have put down her drink just one time, long enough to address the envelope, sign 'Love, Mom,' stick on the stamp and be done with him.

But she hadn't.

Goddamn it all, she hadn't.

And that's all there was to it.

How I Got This Big, Ugly Scar

Nonny reached inside his leather jacket and when his hand came out it was holding a knife. Flicking the blade open, extending his arm, blade up, he declared: "I'm gonna cut you good."

The knife looked bad all right—handle wrapped with black electrician's tape, steel blade scored from sharpening. Must carry a whetstone around to intimidate the other lowlife.

"Yeah," he said after a moment, as if he'd allowed me some time to admire the thing and get good and scared. "I'm gonna give you some of it."

"You bastard!" Lena shouted at him. She was standing there, dressed only in a towel. "Dickless bastard."

He stepped quickly to his left and made a grab to pull her close. But he'd only grasped her towel and it fell away. "Stand still, bitch."

He put an arm around her chest, one of her nipples poking out below his leather-jacketed arm.

"See how sharp this is?"

He touched her wet shoulder with the blade and immediately a red line appeared. Then he pushed Lena away and she tumbled onto the bed.

"I don't think your chickenshit boyfriend's gonna come at me so I'm going to him."

But before he took that first step, Nonny grabbed the quart bottle of Steinlager from the dresser and smashed it against the metal frame of the bed. Green glass and beer sprayed his black jeans and the corner of the bed. Curious, but what I thought was: We didn't finish all that beer?

So he came toward me, broken quart bottle in the left hand, blade in the right. I grabbed Lena's towel from the bed, aware of the open window behind me, traffic sounds out there, smell of frying seafood. I wrapped the towel around my left arm.

He shuffled forward, making little feints with the knife.

When he was close enough, I raised my left arm to protect against any strike and kicked him in the right shin. Nonny stumbled forward and I hit him as hard as I could in the stomach. He fell face first onto the floor, dropping the knife but still holding the beer bottle in his left hand. I stomped on that hand and nudged the bottle away. I bent, turned him over and smashed his face, breaking his nose. Nonny sucked air; then he groaned and then he whimpered.

I straightened up and looked at Lena, naked on the bed, on her knees but leaning back, her small breasts, with the wide brown nipples, swaying gently. Two thin, trickling lines of blood on her right shoulder. One hand was on the metal bedpost, the other on her crotch. She wasn't play-ing with herself but she wasn't far from it.

"Jesus, you surprised me."

"Why?"

"Nonny, he's a bad dude."

"Not that bad."

"It was over so quick," she said.

"I guess I better get him out of here."

She looked at me, held it, started touching herself with her finger.

"Fuck me before you do."

She began to move, lightly, up and down, lifting her ass, dropping it back on her calves while keeping counterpoint with her finger.

The guy muttered. His nose was swollen and spread across his face.

Lena leaned forward and looked down at him.

"Oh," she said. "Oh."

"Hit him again, baby," she said. "Bend down and pop him. Come on. Hit him hard."

"No, I'm getting him out of here."

"Shit. Fucking son-of-a-bitch."

She was rocking harder now.

I dragged Nonny out into the hallway, called downstairs for Herschel, and got him closer to the head of the stairs. The desk clerk looked up. I had a good view of the top of his head. He must not have shaved for a few hours because I could see a dusting of black stubble on top. He arched his eyebrows in a question.

"He bust into the room," I answered. "Came at me with a knife and a broken bottle."

"A knife and a broken bottle. Motherfucker, I'll help you."

I'm not a bad guy. I yanked Nonny's jacket up to protect the back of his head so he wouldn't get a concussion—or another concussion—as we pulled him down the stairs.

Down in the lobby we straightened up, exhaled and regarded him sprawled before us. I noticed we both had our hands on our hips.

"Better drag him out the back," Herschel said. "Leave him in the alley."

"Yeah, what choice do we have?"

"We could feed him to the furnace," he said, and laughed. "Heating bill's outrageous this time of year."

"Can't do that, Hersch. Hotel's got an electric heater."

"Oh, yeah. That's right."

We took him out back.

"Think he'll freeze to death?" Hershel asked, not looking like he gave a shit but that he was mildly curious.

"No, it's dawn in half an hour or so. It'll warm up."

"Yeah."

He closed the back door and we walked to the lobby.

Herschel sat in his aluminum beach chair behind the desk.

"So how's your little friend up there?" he asked.

"What do you mean?"

"Ah, you know."

"Thanks for giving me a hand," I said.

"Yeah, any time."

Lena was collapsed on the bed, arms and legs spread.

"Took you long enough," she said, raising her head. "I came already."

"You got any more left?"

"I got plenty. Come on. That really turned me on. Now I'm getting hot thinking of you fucking me just after beating him. Especially since me and him used to, you know. Same guy doing both's what I mean."

I started taking off my clothes and Lena scuttled backwards, got the bottle of Bailey's from the bedside table, poured some for herself.

"I don't know how you can drink that. At least put some vodka in it."

"No way."

"Well, pour me some vodka."

"You going to be nice to me, stick it wherever I want it?"

"It's a deal."

Lena poured me a drink, handed me the glass, took a big drink from her own and while I was drinking she put her mouth around my thing, flooded it with Bailey's. When the liquor was all gone, she pulled her head away.

"Sure like that," she said. "Cock and Bailey's."

I got into bed.

"Come on. Slap my ass . . . pull my hair . . ."

When we were done, she passed out for a couple of minutes. Woke groggy. Cursed. "Where's my goddamned drink?"

I handed it to her.

"Was there someone pounding on the door?"

"No, you must have dreamed it."

"Ummm, I dreamed he came back. Nonny. He'll be coming after you."

"Maybe, but not for a few days."

"He'll get you. Beat your ass."

"What makes you think he'll be able to do it this time?"

"Because what happened was different."

"Oh."

"I seen him take plenty of guys. All colours."

"Yeah, he's a bad dude, all right."

"You better watch out."

"I will."

"We were pretty solid for a while 'til he got crazy with the powder."

"Yeah, you told me."

And she told me again, only in more detail, going back a couple of years and leading up to him busting through the door just a while ago.

They'd met in a bar when a pimp was promoting her with too much enthusiasm. The guy slapped Lena, and Nonny, playing the hero, saved her. Three months later, she was working the stroll for him. "You know, only for a few weeks. We were in a jackpot."

"I bet."

Their thing was off and on. They'd fight and split, and one of them would go looking, find the other in a bar and start up again.

"You two scrapped a lot, eh?"

"Yeah, we fought. He has a lousy fucking temper."

A month earlier, I'd run into her ex in a place called Don's Wand. I'd heard about him but didn't know what he looked like when he came up to me at the bar. He ordered a beer, paid the guy, turned as if he was taking it back to his table, said, "That Lena you're hanging with? She's bad news, man. Up one minute, down the next. Got a serious fucking temper. I should know. Hope I never see her again. You can have her."

34

He said it like he was permitting me to see her.

Then he sauntered back to where he was sitting with an Indian woman in a sweat suit, and a white guy, a junkie who looked like he was going to fall out of his chair any minute and die on the floor.

So I'd asked her a month before, the first time we went to bed and she told me the story of her love affair with Nonny, "You sure you're done with him?"

"Absolutely. I never want to see the prick again. I want to hang out with you. You're different."

"Yeah, I know that, but how do I know you're not just in-between-times with him?"

"It's been three months. None of the in-between-times ever lasted more than a month."

It wasn't as if I wanted us to go steady, I just didn't fancy being a bit player as their screwed-up love affair unreeled.

We'd had a few disagreements and I'd seen that temper manifest itself a time or two. Once she threw a teapot at me, and a moment later let go with a punch because the teapot had been a birthday gift from her sister and I'd caused her to smash it against the wall. But we had mostly good times. She was smart but she kept much of that hidden. She was very good in bed, too, but she didn't keep that hidden.

"How'd the guy know you were here in the hotel?" I asked her.

"I saw him on the street near the Alhambra. Must have followed me."

Lena drank too much of the Bailey's, went into the bathroom and threw up. I heard the water running as she washed out her mouth.

35

"How do you feel?"

"Better. You're sweet," she said settling into bed, and snuggling against me.

"Feel like doing it again?" she asked.

"As a matter of fact . . . "

"Let's do it real slow this time. Okay?"

"Okay."

A few moments later, she said, "Ooh, I like it that way. Just like that. When you move your body forward like that. Umm. How does it feel to you like that?"

"I like it, honey. It's tight like that."

"Yeah, baby. If it's not tight enough, you can put it somewhere else."

"This is just fine, just like this."

When we were done she settled down to sleep. I reached for my glass, had a sip of vodka. She raised her head for a sip. I tilted the glass to her lips, then she put her head on the pillow. She sobbed and sobbed again. I stroked her hair, and she settled down to whimpering.

"What's the matter, Lena?" I asked as gently as I could.

"He never fucked me like that. Sweet like that. He never knew nothing about fucking, that bastard."

Then she was asleep.

A minute later, I was asleep.

I don't know how long I slept—it might have been two minutes or two hours; probably the latter because weak sunlight was coming in the windows when I was awakened by Lena's hollering and Lena's cursing.

She was hollering and cursing at me.

"You motherfucker, you could have killed him!"

She got out of bed, grabbed her pillow and hit me with it.

36

While her arms were on the upswing, I noticed the vodka bottle was empty which meant she must have woke up and finished it which, in turn, meant she'd finished the Bailey's too.

I was going to hit her back with my pillow, for the hell of it, but I didn't have the energy. She was screaming about how Nonny was a better man than I would ever be. She enumerated my faults and insulted my parents for good measure.

I had been in a deep sleep, having a pleasant dream that I wanted to get back to. There was a cabin in the country with a fireplace and I had a woman there with me who didn't drink Bailey's.

Lena gave no indication of letting up, but she began to recede. I relaxed. Her voice became less distinct after I closed my eyes.

As I was floating back to the cabin in the country, the broken Steinlager bottle ripped into my face, ragged glass slicing me just below the left eye, the pain spreading quick as a snake in a hot broken line to below the corner of my lip.

There was a moment though when I didn't know what had happened and had raised my head, frantic to see what had caused this hurt. I became aware of blood and my first thought was that Nonny had come back; Lena had let him in, and he would be standing in the background admiring his handiwork.

But, no; there she was, naked and light brown as God made her: large nipples, black pubic hair, big brown eyes, Steinlager bottle in her right hand, my blood dripping from it. She stood paralyzed, mouth open. I took hold of a handful of sheet and put it to my face as blood streamed down over my jaw, onto my chest. I was surprised that she had held on to the bottle. You'd think she would have dropped it in shock after sticking it in me, seeing what she'd caused to happen. But no; she stood there watching me for another moment like she didn't know whether to run, apologize, stick me again or masturbate.

She put the bottle down and chose apologizing. Then she started to cry as I looked around for the towel. Her cries turned to wails and I advised her to shut up before somebody called the cops.

"If they show up, we'll have some explaining to do."

Lena brought the towel to me and said sweet things. I told her to get her clothes and get out.

She begged to stay and take care of me. I told her no, to just go.

She didn't argue. I watched her dress, first the sweater, no bra; then her jeans. I have to admit that I took note of her rear end bumping and grinding as she manoeuvered the jeans over her hips. She had panties but hadn't put them on. She got on her boots, her leather jacket, and threw the panties, flimsy pale blue things at me. "Those are to remember me by, you bastard!"

"I already have plenty to remember you by," I said as she slammed the door.

ANOTHER DAY
ON THE BUM

By the side of a stream just west of Medicine Bow, Wyoming, in a depression dug by hand in the dark, is where I'd spent this particular night, spring of 1965, and fitful is how I'd describe my sleep had I got any. If you've ever slept in your clothes by the side of a stream and didn't call it camping, then you probably know what I mean.

I took a long drink of cold water, scooped some of it onto my face, and looked around. It was the Badlands, the Wild West, a two-lane road, not a car nor human in sight. I was free. I was also near broke and past miserable.

I hiked the three miles into Medicine Bow, took a slant on the town and kept on going. Hell, I had one quarter, one nickel and one penny jingling and jangling in my pocket, and I wasn't about to throw them away at the first opportunity. Anyway, I *had* eaten the day before yesterday.

More than breakfast, I was thinking of reaching Denver and calling on Jackie Ann Entwhistle. With any road luck, I'd be in Denver tonight, and if past history could be relied upon as an indicator, I'd be in Jackie Ann's townhouse on the edge of town, rolling around with that tall, slim, red-haired wonder—she of the wondrous rear-end—in her old-fashioned bed. I'd read about a tribe in Africa, where when the chief's son, the prince, required a wife, the custom was to have all the eligible females stand with their heels on a line drawn in the earth. The most desirable female was the one whose posterior stuck out the farthest. Jackie Ann would have been the princess of that tribe, no doubt about it.

I thumbed. The cars whooshed by. No speed limit in Wyoming.

It was hardly more than a year since I'd met Jackie Ann. We'd blown into town, my pal Floyd Wallace and me. He was an adventurer, a rough-hewn intellectual of sorts, who'd shipped all over the world, known Carlo Tresca and Ben Reitman, fought in the Spanish Civil War and various other conflicts. Soon as we arrived in Denver, Floyd rang up Lenore, an old friend—she seemed old to me—who sang country music. She invited us to the roadhouse where she was working and where I met her young friend. Jackie Ann was twenty years younger than Lenore and ten years older than me. I was nineteen.

Everything went as well as could be expected. Hell, it was great. It was near to noon when Floyd began pounding on Jackie Ann's bedroom door, telling me it was time to shake the lead out and hit the road. We were on our way to the annual hobo convention in Britt, Iowa. The Ink Spots were to be the entertainment and we'd see Beefsteak Charlie be crowned King.

40

The sun rose, trucks kicked up dust and grit that stung my face. I thumbed, to no avail. I hiked, threw stones, dreamed big dreams but none, not even the one about thrashing around with Jackie Ann seemed as crazy as having a huge delicious dinner.

Finally, I caught a lift with a construction boss on his way to Laramie, a fellow who, by the looks of him, had that dream-meal of mine as a regular course. He spent his days driving from one site to the next, inspecting the action, checking his clipboard, giving orders, looking at blueprints and pointing. I sat in the truck and watched him at two of these sites. Everybody must have respected him because when I glanced back at knots of workers watching the truck pull away, there didn't seem to be any angry expressions and nobody gave the back of him the finger.

As we drove and talked, I kept looking out of the corner of my left eye at his big scuffed metal lunch box between us on the seat.

He let me out about a mile from the centre of town. My throat was dry. I felt as if my legs would buckle as I trudged along streets with frame houses where dogs were barking on the other side of picket fences.

There were a couple of blocks of board sidewalk and cars and trucks angle-parked along the main drag. There were several restaurants and one of them had a sign in its steamed-up plate glass window touting good old-fashioned home-cooking. I found myself believing the sign, then asking myself what difference it made to the likes of me.

I opened the door to the sounds of conversation and waitress-cook banter, glasses being set down and chairs

41

scraping on the wide-plank floor. Lunchtime in Laramie. There were several tables and a long counter where big men and big women sat before huge meals.

I stood by the cash register taking it all in while I waited for someone to acknowledge me. The person closest to me was a woman working on a leg and a breast of roast chicken—it was golden brown—in a setting of spring potatoes and small tender-looking chunks of carrots. Waiting between the lady's dinner plate and a large glass of iced tea festooned with sprigs of mint, was a bowl of creamy coleslaw.

The guy on the other side of her had a steak. I saw another man with a chicken steak. Waitresses hustled around, plates decorating their arms.

Finally, a large waitress came over to me and her eyeglasses with fake jewel-encrusted rims jumped as she raised her brows in a question. The outside top edges of the glasses flared out in wings and looked dangerous.

"I'll wash dishes or sweep the floors or do anything in exchange for a meal. I can . . ."

"No!" She spit it out and executed a crisp about-face.

I'd read about it, but it had never worked for me in real life.

I took a seat at the counter and began pondering what to order with my thirty-one cents. It was sort of like the indigent's dialectic. I had enough for a coffee and a doughnut or for two doughnuts. But I was too hungry to nibble two doughnuts. They'd be gone in a couple of seconds and I'd have to get out of there. If I just ordered a coffee, I could stop somewhere tonight to rest over another cup. So when a second waitress came past, this one older with carrot-coloured hair, I ordered and she asked me if that was all.

"Yes, ma'am." She gave me a dirty look and went off.

The guy next to me took a forkful of salad—lettuce with shredded carrot and chunks of celery—chewed, swallowed and pushed the bowl away. He'd only eaten half the salad. There were pink liquid traces on the salad that looked like Pepto-Bismol but was probably Russian dressing. Normally, I didn't care for what they called Russian dressing but it looked mighty appealing today.

And there was the waitress, a cup of coffee in one hand, a plate of pork chops swimming in gravy in the other. She slapped down the cup of coffee at my place and gently presented the pork chops to my neighbour. I poured coffee from the saucer back into the cup and watched as he poked with his fork, a broad bean speared on the tines, into the pond of gravy at the top of his mound of mashed potatoes. A gravy tarn on a mashed potato mountain top. Maybe little green peas were resting at the bottom. I looked away.

This other fellow was nearly done a plate of what they called "country spaghetti," the sauce made from mushrooms, tomatoes, onions and peppers. He was working at the remains of the thick sauce with a crusty hunk of bread.

I sipped.

The spaghetti man got up to go, his plate sopped clean, crusts of bread all that remained. Catching the waitress's eye, I raised my cup for a refill. She looked away. The man to my left was reading *Time* magazine and seemed to be picking idly at the remains of his meal, but I couldn't tell for sure because the magazine hid his plate.

43

The waitress passed by.

"Refill?" I said, but she ignored me.

A minute later she was back asking the man with the pork chops if he wanted more coffee. He said no; I said yes; she said, "No refills."

"I thought refills were free."

"You thought wrong."

When my neighbour rolled up the magazine and rose from the counter, I saw an entire plump pork chop remained on his plate, as well as most of his mashed potatoes and half the broad beans. The potatoes and beans and gravy were all mixed together. He took his bill over to the cash register. The underside of my tongue was tingling. I imagined a magnified movie of effervescent hunger explosions, like broad beans erupting from the mashed potato mountain.

He went outside.

I quickly grabbed his plate and pulled it toward me. I *attacked* that pork chop, tearing off a big piece while stabbing at the vegetable mash. Oh, lord. Lord, it was good.

The chop was most important so I worked on that first, getting a second piece halfway down before hazarding a look around. The women hadn't noticed. Some old rancher with a prune face had but I ignored him, hunkered down and continued at it.

"Hey!"

I didn't look up, smelled perfume coming closer. "Hey, what the hail you think you're doin?"

I took another swallow before looking up. It was the one with the orange hair. "Eating," I said, and ate.

"You didn't pay for that there food!"

She was joined by the larger lady with the rhinestone

44

glasses. Years later I would always think of her when I saw pictures of Divine in the John Waters films.

"I said, you didn't pay for that there food."

They both had their hands on their hips, palms outward.

"This meal has already been paid for."

"But not by you, you bum."

"What difference does that make?"

"That you're a bum? Who wants . . ."

"No, what difference does it make that I wasn't the one who paid for it? You've made your money off the meal."

"I'm going to call the law and have you arrested."

Since it wouldn't have been polite to answer with a mouthful of food, I waited until I had swallowed another substantial fork's worth before asking, "For what?"

"For stealing from us."

"But I didn't steal it. First of all it's not yours anymore since you sold it to that man."

"Harlen. *He's* no bum."

"Harlen. You'd have to go fetch him, convince him to lay a charge against me, although it wouldn't stand up because he was finished with his meal, walked away evidently satisfied, thereby relinquishing any claims on the remaining food. One meal, one payment. Says so right in the Wyoming Criminal Code, jurisprudence section, that clause about restaurant mores."

"You're from the city. You ain't from Wyoming."

"Anyway, if it's paid for twice, *you're* the one'd be stealing. Not only that, there's the health department to think of."

"We're calling the boss."

45

I concentrated on the food, finished, stood and sauntered out of there, real casual-like yet aware of hostile looks from legitimate patrons.

When half a block away, I glanced over my shoulder and saw a man standing by the door in white pants, white T-shirt, dirty apron, looking in my direction, trying to nail me to the boardwalk with his baleful stare.

I walked faster, thinking about those cops who couldn't arrest me for stealing but might easily nail me on a vagrancy charge.

Before reaching the outskirts of the business district I got a lift to Cheyenne with a young guy in a '48 Plymouth. Two more rides took me into Fort Collins, and another, to downtown Denver. The plan was to clean up, and then, with my last dime, phone Jackie Ann.

When I walked into the bus station, my spirit was soaring. There was a mural of the Rocky Mountains across the washroom walls and there I was gliding over Pike's Peak. There was also a mirror and I made the mistake of looking in it, my spirit immediately plummeting, until it lay in the dirty grout between the scuffed tiles of the washroom floor. I was grimy and sunburned, greasy hair down to my shoulders, dirt under my nails and in the creases of my fingers. I didn't smell so great either. The lady in Laramie was right; I was a bum.

Dragging myself back into the waiting room, I found a pinball machine to lean against and mope. People were buying tickets and looking up at the big board. It all seemed so futile. What was the use of going anywhere or doing anything? My luck had finally run out.

I didn't know what to do, didn't feel like doing anything.

Way down low, I was, in the Mile High City.

Then opportunity presented itself over by the bus station doors, in the form of a guy in his twenties who looked even worse than I did. Dressed in an old pair of green work pants, work boots, and the too-small jacket from a striped seersucker suit, he was accosting people and importuning. The people were offended, often pivoting like halfbacks to get around him. I assumed he was a panhandler until I noticed him waving a watch at some old farmer's dewlap.

I sashayed over in his direction and when fifteen feet away, he moved on me like Groucho Marx. "Wanna buy a watch? Hunnert dollar watch, my friend; you can have it for ten!"

"You got the wrong guy."

The sides of his head were shaved, the patch of black hair at the top looked as if it had been swept off the barbershop floor and glued on. His jacket pockets were lumpy with what must have been wristwatches. He jabbed the watch at me, "Guaranteed for life!"

"Does bubblegum come with it?"

"Whattaya mean?"

He had small brown eyes like cigarette burns and there were food traces at the corners of his mouth. He slipped a hand through the watchband, banged the face of it into the palm of his other hand.

"See, still ticking," he said.

"Thank you, John Cameron Swayze."

"Huh?"

"Sell many?"

"Dozens. But not to tightwads like you."

"Gee, you got a great sales technique."

"Think you could do better?"

"I *know* I could do better."

"Yeah, yeah. You could sell iceboxes to —"

"Don't say it. Listen, I tell you what." I smiled at him but it wasn't easy. "I'll sell the watches for you."

"Go'way. You're wasting my time."

"You give me half of each one I sell."

"Whattaya think I am?"

"I'll pretend you didn't ask. Hey, let me help you. Help both of us."

"I paid good money for these."

"Bullshit. You boosted them; what do I care? Look, I've been watching and I know you haven't sold wristwatch one. What've you got to lose? Hand one over and pay attention."

I snatched the watch from his fingers. "Thanks. Let me have another one."

We were kind of like brothers of bumdom. Dirty fingers our secret Masonic sign.

I took a few steps and he was right with me.

"Stand back, my man. I don't want them to think we're together."

An over-aged juvenile delinquent was coming out of the men's room. He stopped to light a cigarette, did so with cupped hands, and put the pack back in a rolled T-shirt sleeve. He had a tattoo on his left forearm.

"Hey, man," I said, coming up to him, looking around. "I got these watches. Take a look." I took another glance, left and right. "Bulls'll be through in a minute or two."

He blew smoke out of the right side of his mouth and closed his right eye to a slit.

48

"Yeah, sure. Fuckin' bulls."

"New in town. Got a dozen watches, got to get rid of 'em. They go for a yard a piece in a store. Check this one out."

I handed him the one with a gold band and he checked it out like an old guy in the Jura Mountains. He looked like the kind of dude who'd just done six months on a B&E charge and was revelling in the experience now that it was over.

"You can have it for ten."

He reached into a front pocket of his tight black jeans and came up with a roll, peeled a sawbuck off the top.

"Here, man."

"Thanks, pal."

"Hang tough."

He strode off, thumbs hooked in his pockets, and I gave the ten to the goof. He looked at it in disbelief, turning it over in his grubby paws.

"Now let me have a couple of more—one a ladies. And you just sit over there like a good capitalist while I earn you money."

It was easy. I sold five more in an hour. My pitch was innovative, creative and sounded sincere; naturally, it changed with the prospective client. I sold an elegant number to somebody's dear sweet grandmother. One each to a pair of black teenaged guys. I envisioned making a career out of this. Well, maybe not a career; it would be a stepping stone to bigger things. Somebody would alert the papers and they'd write me up. It would become the thing to do: fall by the bus station and buy a watch from me.

There was that damned fantasizing again. What always got me in trouble. More likely, I'd last another forty-five minutes before getting busted. I got my thirty-dollar share from the goof and split. It was still only eight o'clock. Enough time to eat, clean up and go see Jackie Ann.

Eating could wait. I checked the phone book. She was still at her place in Cherry Hill. Best to surprise her, just appear on her doorstep. I had a shower at the YMCA and changed into my other pants and shirt, bought a half-dozen roses and found the local bus to her place.

Her area was all medium-rise apartment buildings and new townhouses. Everything looked like it had been scrubbed and landscaped by anal-retentives. No crumbling red brick and Larimer Street winos out there. I knocked on her door. My heart was pounding. I heard footsteps. The door opened.

Same red hair and strange light blue eyes. She looked so good, my insides did a somersault. Jackie Ann stared for a second before recognizing me. "What are *you* doing here?"

"I came to see you. Gee, you look great, Jackie Ann."

"I'm sorry, I forget your name."

She overdid it but I said my name. I asked about Lenore. She said Lenore was fine. Still singing? Still singing. I extended the roses but she didn't reach for them. She gave me a quick look up and down but not in the way she had the year before. "I suppose you're still drifting around."

"Yes, I guess so. I've just come from California."

"What do you expect to accomplish?"

I didn't tell her what my first goal was, one I realized I might not achieve.

"Are you going to invite me in?"

"No." She sighed and her shoulders rose and fell, her breasts too. "What would be the point to it?"

"Well . . ."

"I don't hear from you for nearly a year and then here you are on my doorstep."

"Okay."

"You're going to wind up a bum in the park."

"Maybe so."

I turned and started along the walkway. One step, two steps. She'd call me back. I knew she would. Jackie Ann had to say those things and pretend she had forgotten my name so she could justify letting some drifter back into her house, and into her bed.

I reached the pavement.

Nothing.

The door slammed.

I trudged toward the bus stop with my roses.

There was a lady walking a dog.

"Madame, for you."

She was a pleasant-looking woman, in her late forties—fifty at most—walking a white fluffy dog.

I handed her the flowers. She was startled for a moment, but smiled and took them with good grace. The runt of a dog looked up at me and trembled.

I sat on the bench to wait for the bus. I'd go back into town and find a skid row hotel room with the usual sagging bed. Just where I belonged. Ten minutes went by.

A car pulled up to the curb. The driver looked at me and smiled. "That was a sweet thing you did."

At first I didn't realize who it was.

"The flowers. Would you like to come with me?"

I walked over to the car and got in. She gave me a sort of mischievous look. Her skirt was a few inches above her

51

knees. Her legs were just a bit plump, but appealingly so. She wore sheer stockings and she smelled good. I patted the dog. The lady made a U-turn and we were on our way.

JOHN THE BAPTIST

For a year I was the superintendent at 56 Howland Avenue in Toronto, in a neighbourhood that came to be known as the Annex. It seems like everyone who took a room at the place was a character, but the strangest of all was the guy I called John the Baptist. I called him that because that's how he introduced himself.

One day, I'm sitting on the steps talking to my buddy Marcel Horne who was the super next door at 54. We were actually remembering unusual people we'd bumped into in our travels. Fate was sending another one to us, and he was only a few yards away.

Marcel and I spent a lot of time like that, hanging out, cutting up jackpots, retrieving bits of the past. And all the while, this day, we could hear Jack Dennison in the backyard next door at 58, singing. We could tell by his voice he hadn't had more than a few. He was moving his rainspouts around, singing his favourite: *"Crying's not for me. You'll never stop the rain by complaining . . ."*

A man was turning onto the walkway of 56, just as we looked up.

He was in his early thirties, dressed in a brown monk's robe pulled snugly at the hips with a length of rope, and carrying an old-fashioned doctor's bag. He was medium height and thickly built, swatches of tangled brown hair visible under the woolen hood.

When he reached the steps where we were sitting, the man pressed his hands together at his chest and bowed. "I've come to inquire about a room," he said, looking from one of us to the other.

"I'm the super," I said, "so inquire away."

He nodded his head.

"You can do what you want here as long as you don't bother your neighbour."

"Of course."

"No loud music."

"I have no music."

"No drugs."

Marcel tried to stifle a laugh, and it wound up being a loud snort.

"No drugs."

"You want to see the room that's available?"

"Yes, please."

Evening was falling and the robed man carrying the doctor's bag followed me like a monk returning just in time for vespers. I took him to room six on the second floor. Adeline in room five, having heard strange footsteps in the hallway, peeked out her door. She was just about the darkest person I'd ever seen. Getting a load of the guy I was bringing up to be her neighbour, she looked at me and rolled her eyes before ducking back into the room.

"It's not much," I said, opening the door to number six. "But it's not expensive either."

There was a single bed, a small table and ladderback chair, an armchair, and a large dresser. The floor was covered in linoleum and the window offered a side view of the brick house next door.

"I really don't need the cushioned chair."

"Bathroom's down the hall. It's got a big tub, but no shower. There's a shower downstairs. You want to see it?"

"No, that's fine."

"You share it with two other people."

He nodded, and brought money from the folds of his garment.

"Thank you," he said. "I have everything I need."

I removed the armchair and took it upstairs to the El Salvadorean couple who were hiding out in the attic. Then I rejoined Marcel on the steps.

He looked up at me quizzically, the usual shy and wry smile on a face that was already grizzled at thirty-three.

"I guess if you wanted to do something strange," Marcel said, "you could rent a room to a regular person."

"You rented a room to a regular person once. Remember the guy who worked at the insurance office? And he's the only one that ever stiffed you for the rent."

"Never again."

Marcel was a firebreather. He spent years working the carnivals but now he was performing a more elaborate version of his act on theatre stages—when he could get work. A year-and-a-half earlier I had lived in the same front room at 54 Howland that he was in now and I had been the super there too. Both sides of the duplex were owned by a family called Brinbaum who had other properties in Toronto. The managers of 54 and 56 were first cousins named Jay and Lorne, and one of them came by each week to collect the rents. They never even stepped inside their places, didn't want to. As long as they got their money they didn't care who we rented rooms to—with one exception.

The one exception was Jack Dennison, the singing tinsmith. Lorne and Jay had taken an instant and intense dislike to Jack who, although an often hopeless drunk, was also the nicest man in the neighbourhood. He was in his forties and handsome when sober. He'd been married with a young daughter and had made a good living at his trade. Six years before I met him, Jack's daughter had been picked off the street on her way to school. Five days later, a hiker found her bloated body snagged by a log in the Humber River. She had been raped repeatedly. Her killer was never found.

Jack's marriage didn't survive the tragedy. His wife left and he gave up his job in favour of drinking.

Now, he spent most of his days on the street or in the yard singing. Many nights in his basement room at 58, you could hear him weeping.

To Jay and Lorne though, Jack was just a pathetic loser. Jay was thin; Lorne was taller and heavy-set. Neither were more than twenty-five. They were in their suits, white shirts and ties, week after week, winter or summer. They thought I was crazy living the way I did, just scraping by, when so far as they could tell I was neither a drug addict, alcoholic or any sub-species of white trash. They couldn't fathom that I was doing what I wanted to do or had to do. Although they didn't know for sure who lived in their houses, they had an idea it wasn't anybody from the board of directors at the Young Men's Hebrew Association a couple of blocks away.

"There's liable to be trouble," Jay told me. "The sort of people you rent to."

"For the service you're providing, what do you expect?"

They didn't know how much rent people were paying, either, although they thought they did. I rented each room for five bucks more than I told the cousins. The extra money made up for the rent I wasn't charging the Salvadoreans, and for such things as the space heater I'd put in their third-floor garret, which had no other heat. The Salvadoreans had made an epic journey from their country, a journey that had taken nearly two years, much of it on foot. They'd arrived in Toronto with one name and the name sent them to me.

I also had a little hustle going with the Weiner brothers who owned a hardware store on Bloor Street, just east of Howland. They would write me inflated receipts when I needed parts for repairs, and I'd kick back a few dollars. This plus the occasional day labouring job, and a book review here and there allowed me to get by. My rent was free.

More importantly, I was free or so I thought. I wasn't renting my body out for eight hours of drudgery and I wasn't a hack writer, deluding myself that I was financing my great novel. I was free to scrape by and relish the life of the street.

A week after I rented the room to John the Baptist, I ran into Adeline at a grocery store on Bloor. "You know, that man in the room next to me sure is unusual."

"Does he give you a hard time?"

"He don't bother me but sometimes I think I hear noises like people in there whispering."

"Maybe it *is* people in there whispering."

"Don't never hear nobody coming in and go out."

"Well you work all day, Adeline. Maybe they leave after you go to work. Our Prime Minister said we shouldn't be too concerned about what goes on in the bedrooms of the nation."

"Shee-it. You ought to come up to my room tonight and listen. See what you make of it."

Adeline laughed.

"Colonel might get jealous."

She laughed some more and faked a grab at my crotch. The Italian greengrocer gave us the *mal occhio*.

I had nodded hello to the monk a couple times but only talked to him once that first week. One afternoon, I saw him sitting at a table in the little strip of park that ran east and west along the top of the subway line between Bathurst and Howland. There were three little kids around him, two sitting on top of the table, the other one standing close to him. He had his brown bag of papers in front of him. John was talking, holding one page in one hand, waving his pen with the other hand like he was conducting a choir, a choir of little kids.

The next day I asked him how he liked his room; he said it was fine and quoted a snippet of scripture.

"I notice you use the fire escape more than you do the front door."

He shrugged, looked sheepish.

"It doesn't matter to me," I told him.

I had the big front room on the first floor. Across the

hall and facing the house next door was a smaller room occupied by Janine, a Christian Science hooker. The tenant before her was a woman who'd made the mistake of marrying a gypsy. Her husband's family wouldn't allow her into the circle and wouldn't allow him to live with her. He kept her stashed in the little room for a couple of months, visiting a couple of times a week. One night when he was there some other gypsies came over and took him away, not without a lot of scuffling. It was my job to try and put a stop to the fracas but I didn't think my appearance on the scene would be welcome. Hell, I thought all of them would turn on me. But they didn't. They didn't want a hassle with the *gadja* world. They took the traitor away and he never came back. The woman left the next week, headed, she said, to Sudbury.

So Janine replaced her. She was short, pale and rounded though curvaceous. She reminded me of a Butterball turkey before it went into the oven. Janine spent most of each day in her room reading tracts or hanging around the temple on Spadina Road. Nights, she'd cruise Bloor Street, places like the Manhattan Café, for older men to bring back to the room.

Down the hallway from our rooms was a kitchen, bath and empty back room. The second floor had its own kitchen and bath, so whenever Janine heard water running on the first floor she knew it was me. A few times when I was taking a shower, she walked right in—the bathroom door didn't lock—and stepped into the shower stall with me, naked.

"Janine. Go back to your room. We've been through this before."

"Oh, don't be like that."

"Go away."

"I bet I can do it better than that skinny bitch you had in your room last week."

"Janine, thanks but no thanks. Let me take my shower in peace."

She walked back and forth down the hall that way all the time—naked. It didn't concern her in the least who might be coming in or going out. That's how she was one afternoon when John the Baptist saw her.

"He's creepy," Janine told me. "He kept looking at my breasts and my bush."

The latter was the same colour as her hair, a natural bright orange.

"He's a religious nut and I wouldn't be surprised if you were a great temptation to him."

"He didn't proposition me though. Just started to preach. I got around him and back to my room but I felt him watching me. Then the next day he knocked on my door and when I opened it he did some more preaching, all the time staring at my titties. I closed the door on him but it doesn't stop. I wish you would say something to him."

"I will."

That night I went upstairs with the intention of speaking to John, but just as I was about to knock, I heard small muffled voices that made me think of fairies or trolls. I was turning away when Adeline cracked open her door and motioned me inside.

"You hear that? Man's in there with who knows what all or who all."

"Well, what does it matter?"

"It ain't right."

"What ain't right?"

"Whatever it is he's doing."

"You hear any screams or blood-curdling yells?"

"Not yet, but they're coming."

"Better mind your own business, Adeline." I looked toward her dresser. She kept it polished, a lace doily over the top, a few bottles on there and a white plastic Colonel Sanders coin bank. The first time I'd gone up to collect rent from her, Adeline noticed me noticing the Colonel and she broke out in embarrassed giggles which only increased when she realized I realized the extra duty done by the Colonel. "You better hope John the Baptist doesn't hear you and the Colonel!"

She grabbed a pillow and hit me with it.

"Get yourself down here on this bed and we can have a pillow fight, and who knows what else."

Adeline reminded me of one of those matronly black religious ladies I used to see as a kid in Virginia. Hair all pomaded until it looked like a stiff pillow sitting on the back of her head, black-rimmed glasses, three or four gold teeth, dresses down almost to her ankles, and stout shoes like turn-of-the-century suffragettes used to wear.

She got rid of the long dress, the stout shoes and began the ritual of removing the elaborate system of pins that held the bun in place. When she was finished, she patted the bed, "Come on, honey. The Colonel needs a rest tonight, but Adeline don't."

The next morning I stopped John the Baptist as he was going out for his morning walk.

"Good tidings!" he said by way of greeting.

"Same to you. But, listen, I've had a complaint. I just want to tell you that it's not right to pester people with your beliefs."

"But it's my job, my mission, to spread the word—the good tidings that the Messiah is about to appear."

"Well don't go knocking on people's doors to tell them, at least not at 56 Howland."

"But it's of the greatest significance."

"Maybe not to them."

"I know what the red-headed lady does. And the tall man who brings harlots back at night. And you . . . "

"What any of us do is none of your business unless we interfere with you. And vice versa."

"John the Baptist spread his teaching in the enemy camp."

"Yeah, well, I'm sure the enemy has many camps, and if you keep it up you're going to have to find another one of them. There's probably one on Albany Avenue."

The back room on the second floor was never officially rented yet was occupied most nights. My brother Dave stayed there two or three times a week, other nights it would be one of the Kaljus, two Estonians who hated each other, or Denny, the emcee at the Brunswick House who'd bring back one of his groupies.

What with all these people coming and going, me dealing with their problems and requests, trying to get some writing done, doing dumb jobs for a few bucks and tending to my social life, I wasn't keeping close tabs on the Baptist. Of course, it never occurred to me to keep close tabs on him or anyone else in the house. I didn't interfere in anyone's life. That's how I explained it to the cops, and it was true.

One day I got a job moving stoves and refrigerators from a boxcar to a truck to a store in the suburbs. It wasn't easy work and probably still isn't. At five-thirty, one of the guys I'd been on the job with dropped me off on the south side of Bloor near the Castle Frank station. Who should I see scurrying across the road that wound up from the Parkway but John the Baptist himself. He was holding a little girl no more than seven years old in one arm, and had his doctor's bag in his other hand. He ran with his sandals slapping the asphalt and his hems flipping up to reveal his chubby white legs. When he got to the other side of the exit road, he set the little girl down on the grass, took her hand and they walked several yards until they were adjacent to the subway entrance where they both sat on the ground.

I watched from the other side of the street. After about five minutes had passed, a car pulled over, and John and the little girl stood up. A man was driving. John bent down and the little girl kissed him on the forehead. He straightened up, opened the car door and the girl got in. After the car pulled away, I waited for an opening and dashed across Bloor Street.

"Yo, John!"

"Greetings, brother!" he called.

As I got closer, I saw that his robes and sandals were wet, bits of grass stuck to the tops of his feet.

"Hey, John. You been down to the river baptising souls?"

"Indeed, I have. For am I not John, the son of Elizabeth and Zacharias, come from Bethuraba to cleanse folks of their sins in the waters of the Jordan?"

"Where're you really from?"

"Paris. The one in Ontario."

We rode together to the Bathurst stop. My lack of antagonism encouraged him to preach, and as he did so his enthusiasm increased, so that by the time we reached St. George he was waving his chubby hands around and most of the other riders were giving him their attention. There was a gleam in his eye, and I thought I detected some humour there, like a funny glint amongst the gleam. Like he was aware of himself, aware his preaching was on the verge of being *schtick*.

The way the riders looked at John reminded me a bit of the reaction "Subway Elvis" got. He was a guy who'd roamed the subways up until a couple of years earlier. He dyed his hair, first black, later blond, and wore '50s greaser outfits. He'd be sitting, ostensibly minding his own business on a cold winter morning, and then stand up, lay a stare on some poor white-collar commuter, and shout, *"You looking for trouble? Just look in my face."*

And he'd go through the whole of "King Creole," complete with swivelling hips, pouts and snarls and brooding stares.

People didn't look away. It was fascinating.

They regarded John in the same manner.

We left the subway and walked along the laneway at the back of the Bloor Street stores, adjacent to the strip of park over the subway line. I could hear Jack Dennison from two blocks away. He was sitting on the bench at Howland with his bottle in a bag: *"Raindrops keep falling on my head . . ."*

Two little girls and a little boy were playing in the park and as we walked by, they called out: "It's John the Baptist! Hi John!"

I studied him as he smiled and waved at the kids. There didn't seem to be anything in his face but friendliness.

He's just a harmless nut, I thought.

As we turned onto Howland, Jack Dennison raised his head from his brown paper bag, nodded at me and glared at the monk.

"Peace unto you, brother," John said.

"Fuck you, pervert."

It worried me, Jack saying that. On the one hand, I told myself that he was in his cups and liable to say anything to anybody. But, then again, maybe Jack's terrible experience allowed him the ability to detect some secret.

Two days later, Adeline told me she'd woken up in the middle of the night and thought she'd heard voices in the bathroom down the hall. "Sounded like a little girl in there, and a man. Must have been that creep in the next room. You ought to go to the cops."

"Me?"

We were in her room, in her bed, lying on our sides facing each other.

"Yeah, mon. You the super."

I got out of bed and walked over to the window. Jack was in the yard next door, dragging eavestroughs around, arranging them in some kind of order that made sense to him. When he was on a binge, Jack was given to pulling down eavestroughs and rainspouts and dragging them back to the yard. On sober days, he'd go back to the same houses, say that he'd been walking by and noticed the missing metal work and he just happened, by sheer coincidence, to be a tinsmith and would be glad to install a replacement for a pittance of what it would cost if someone who wasn't a neighbour did the job.

65

"And what do I tell them?" I asked Adeline. "To arrest John the Baptist because you heard voices in the bathroom and you knew one of the voices was his?"

"Well, something is going to happen for sure."

What worried me even more was that Jack Dennison had called John the Baptist a pervert, and had done so with pure hate in his voice. Jack never had a bad word for anyone unless that someone was a cop.

I got dressed and went down to the yard of 58. Jack was stone sober, bathed and shaved, long brown hair combed back.

"Why'd you call him that? You remember?"

"Yeah, I remember saying it. He gives me the creeps. It's like I look at him and I can see into his evil heart."

"You ever see him before?"

"No, never before. But I *know*."

I saw John leave the house late the next morning. He had his doctor's bag, so I knew he wasn't just going down to the corner store. Jack was still sober so I enlisted him to stand watch while I went up the fire escape and into the monk's room. I had checked out the hall door but found he had stuck a paper match in the slit between the top of the door and the jamb. I was afraid if I opened the door, I wouldn't get the match back in the right place, and that he'd notice.

A towel was on the ladderback chair. Soap, toothbrush and paste on the dresser; a pencil and a drinking cup on the table. In the dresser were a change of underwear and two pairs of woolen socks; a pair of work boots were the only things in the closet. He evidently had no clothes of any kind. There was nothing under his bed or under his pillow; nothing between the sheets and the bedspread, nor between the mattress and box spring. The room didn't have a rug for him to hide anything under, but it did have an old oval mirror, clouded at the edges, that was attached to the dresser, and covered at the back with brown paper. The paper was so brittle I thought it must have been on the mirror when it was purchased. There was a slit in the paper at the left rear of the mirror and inside the slit, between the paper and the mirror, were five Polaroid pictures of little girls. There was nothing pornographic about the pictures, although the girls seemed to have been posed in a manner that might be deemed provocative. One girl was photographed from behind, bending over by the side of a river to pick up a stone, her face turned to smile at the camera. Another was shown on a pier at a lake, it was as if she had changed into a new outfit after swimming, a pleated cotton skirt, like a tennis skirt, and a white blouse. The little girl sat with crossed legs, skirt up her thighs, three buttons undone on her blouse. If these photos provoke you, I could hear a defense attorney declare, you must be the one with the problem.

I put the photographs back and went out the window. Jack wanted to know what I'd found and I told him I hadn't found anything.

My next move was to go see a lawyer I knew who would give me advice without me having to give him any money. Although he's dead now, this man became rather well known as an entertainer so I won't mention his name or why he owed me a favour.

"A couple more months," he said, "and all this will be a memory."

He made a sweep with one small arm to indicate the office with his degrees on the wall.

"You're busy, eh?"

"Yes. I think I have a regular part in a series."

I told him about my suspicions. He told me I needed something more to take to the cops.

"If you were more of a—how shall I say this . . . regular citizen, the cops might put a half-hearted tail on the guy, check out his background—but you're not. A regular citizen, I mean. And I'm sure you don't want any heat coming down on that joint where you're holed up."

That's the way he talked, like he was auditioning. He had a point though. If the cops fell by the rooming house, they were liable to haul in the lot of us.

Three days later, eleven in the morning, I was sitting at my desk trying to do some work when I looked out the front window and saw the monk going down the steps. Without thinking about it, I got up to follow him.

He had his doctor's bag and he walked hurriedly down the sidewalk. When he turned into the laneway in back of Bloor, I knew he was going to the subway. There was no one else in the lane or the park, so if John turned around he would see me. I went down to Bloor, turned and hurried west until I got to Bathurst and down into the subway before he did. I followed him onto an eastbound train, stayed a car behind, and got off when he did at Castle Frank.

He never looked back as he crossed the road, went down the hill and along the river. He stopped by some bushes, sat on a rock and took his papers and a carton of milk out of his bag. He drank some milk from the carton and scribbled on his papers, me watching from behind a few scraggly trees a hundred yards away.

After half an hour, a woman came along with a little girl of about nine or ten years old. She had thick black hair and the colour of her skin made me think she was Mexican or Central American. John and the woman were talking about the girl, I could tell by their gestures. The woman patted the girl on the head and John nodded. Then the woman patted the girl on her rear end. John stood up from his rock, took something from the folds of his garment and handed it to the woman who nodded her head once, turned and walked off.

John put his hands on the girl's shoulders and urged her down onto the rock. He sat down beside her and brought some pastry from his bag to give to her. They sat like that for several minutes, John talking to her, and then he stood up and took her hand. He left his doctor's bag on the ground and they started walking. I started down the slope after them.

When I got to the path by the Don River they weren't in sight at first and then I picked up some movement in the bush. I saw them for a moment before they disappeared in a thick copse of trees. They were completely out of sight of anyone who happened to be walking by, completely secluded in the big city.

I went toward them as quietly as possible. In a couple of minutes, I could hear the monk's voice. I heard him say, "I bring you good tidings."

I had been trying to prepare myself for whatever I'd see, but it didn't work. I brushed aside the last curtain of branches and there was the little girl, naked now, leaning against a large stone, and John with his robes hiked up, knees bent, and his short, thick dick nuzzling the girl's rear end.

He jumped back at the noise, fear in his eyes, mouth open. He put his hands up like I had a gun on him, the brown wool of his garment folded over his dick. John the Baptist started whimpering.

"God forgive me," he said.

"If he does," I answered, "you can keep him."

I didn't feel any outrage or anger. I felt almost numb and like I was doing everything in slow motion. John didn't horrify me, but the little girl did. She straightened up and faced me, naked with a blank expression on her face.

"Put on your dress," I told her.

"Don't you want to fuck me, too?"

"No."

She made a clicking sound with her tongue and a quick shrug of her shoulders.

"I was going to baptize us both," John said. "Cleanse us of our sins."

"You were going to do that afterwards, right?"

"Yes, the only thing that feels as good as young pussy is the healing power of running water."

"How much time'd you do in the joint?"

"Altogether?"

"Yeah."

"Five years. Different bits."

"You get religion there?"

"Yeah."

"Let's get moving."

He didn't resist.

"I sensed that you were onto me," he said.

"Yeah."

"You and the wino."

"He could smell it on you."

"Where d'you think you're taking me?"

"Up the hill and we're going to wait for the first cruiser."

"No, you're not."

"What're you going to do? Scrap with me? You think you can beat me?"

"No, I'm going for the water."

"What? You're going to get away by swimming?"

"I'm not going to swim."

"You think if you go back to prison they're going to behead you like they did your namesake?"

"Fuck, no, man. I'll be out in six months. You didn't see me actually do anything. My word against yours. I could say you were about to plug her. The hell with it. I'm gone into the water. Don't stop me. It's best all around."

He headed for the Don. A few steps in, he looked around at me. "In my room, in back of the mirror. There's photographs. Sweet young pussy, man. The one on the pier at Wasaga Beach. It's the wino's daughter. See you."

"See you."

He walked halfway out into the river. It seemed too shallow for what he wanted to do, but then with one step the monk disappeared. He didn't come up.

I waited there on shore, holding the girl's hand so she wouldn't run away.

"Who was the woman who brought you to that man?"

"I don't know. She bought me from some other woman."

I waited fifteen, twenty minutes. There was no sign of him.

"Come on, little girl. Let's go."

"I'm not a little girl."

"Yeah, I guess not."

We went up the hill and I flagged a cab near the subway station. I didn't particularly care for cops, but I told the driver to call them.

She Still Turns
My World
Upside Down

It was a Saturday night in St. Augustine. I'd gotten into town the day before, having fled a Toronto winter and a bad romance. We both knew it was over, had known it was over, and all I saw in the future—if I stayed—were weeks or months more of the kind of bickering that ate at the soul and turned old lovers into bitter enemies. At least that's how I explained it to her and myself.

So there'd been three days driving down, mostly on the Interstate after crossing the border, one entire driving day devoted to observing the signs for South of the Border, one hundred yards below the South Carolina line, a genuine American success story, an empire that began in the '50s as a tacky peanut brittle stand and grew to the vast tacky tourist trap it was now. I'd even stopped there, walked around, looked at souvenirs and entire families of Ohioans eating ice cream cones, and tried to picture her up there in Toronto taking cabs to parties where she and all her friends talked about Mies Van der Rohe and Le Corbusier. It was always that way whenever we went to a party with her friends; they spoke of the famous architects Mies and Corbu as if they were old and intimate friends.

I checked into a motel on the highway where we'd once spent a week together. True, I could have tried somewhere else but I told myself I wasn't sentimental, just tired of driving. It was a different room though, right across from the one we'd had, over by the oleander and the ice machine. Back then I'd had a white Lincoln Continental with a blue top and blue leather upholstery. When the week was over, we'd made a deal. She took the Lincoln and left, drove to New Orleans, and I didn't see her for a year. I truly forget what I got as my part of the deal.

Anyway, this time, I spent the next morning searching for a place to live and found a trailer in a little park on San Marco Boulevard. The rest of the day I hung around town, looked up a couple of acquaintances, did some shopping and settled in. At night, I went across the road to a bar I'd drunk in once or twice in the past. I remembered being fond of the Spanish Armada because, unlike other bars in town, it was accepting of everyone. I mean, you had your redneck dives, tourist places festooned with nets and buoys, and cocktail lounges catering to the small white-collar crowd. The Armada was a mix of all that.

I noticed him right away. Or rather I heard loud laughter over by the jukebox, turned and saw this lean raw-boned fellow in the middle of three other people, his head thrown back, laughing like he'd just heard the funniest joke ever heard by any good old boy south of South of the Border. Actually, it was the laugh of someone who liked to laugh and was used to doing it. His friends, two women and a man, laughed with him. Hell, it was infectious. I noticed the bartender-proprietor was snickering too, giving them his attention, though I was only a couple of feet away and wanting a drink. I remembered him too, an old boozer. Now and again, over the years, people, probably other drunks, had told him he looked a little like Robert Mitchum. I wondered whether that had inspired him to keep his eyelids permanently at half-mast or whether it was natural.

The barkeep finally noticed me, shook his head. "That Darrell. Boy sure likes to party hardy. What'll it be?"

I drank bourbon on the rocks in those days. He brought it over, adding, "But he's got what you'd call a mercurial temper. Say, you've been in here before."

"Yeah, but not for a couple of years. Been up in Canada."

"Well, you're always welcome. Anyway, what I mean is that Darrell is a regular old life-of-the-party one minute and the next he's so low he looks like he's about to bawl his eyes out."

The Spanish Armada began to fill up and I forgot about the guy who'd been laughing. My neighbour from the trailer park came over and I got acquainted with him. He was a northerner who'd retired and come down to spend the rest of his life fishing. He was the kind of guy who'd roll out of bed in the morning, put on his shorts and flip-flops, pick up his gear and head for the beach or the pier. Florida was full of men just like him. At night, he added a T-shirt to the ensemble and went across the road for a drink and some companionship.

A little later, a guy sitting at a table with his girl waved to me, and I went over. I'd met him the last time I'd been in St. Augustine. He ran the local archives all by himself. Quite a job, since the material had been piling up since 1612.

Or he used to run it himself.

"I got a part-time assistant now."

"Yeah, you sure do," said his ladyfriend, rolling her eyes.

"Darling, I just take what they give me."

"Yeah, right. I just wonder how much she gives you."

He looked embarrassed. I'd always thought he might be gay.

Once she finished teasing him, we resumed a conversation we'd been in the middle of the last time I'd seen him. He'd been interested in the fact that I'd lived in the Yukon. In fact, the first time I met him, I'd come directly to St. Augustine from Dawson City. He was convinced that Robert Services's Lady named Lou had wound up in this little north Florida town, after a stint running a brothel in San Francisco.

Anyway, we talked about things and somebody played some Gary Stewart on the jukebox, and the archivist's ladyfriend asked me to dance. I looked at him and he told me sure, to go ahead. Well, if you're at a roadhouse, the person you want on the jukebox is Gary Stewart or someone like him. I don't know what happened, but for a while there Gary Stewart was the best thing in the country music business, his songs covering the whole range from wild rocking to serious hurting with plenty of sly humour thrown in at all the right times. Somebody else on the floor was a big fan and had played all the Stewart songs on the box. The first three were fast numbers and everybody was dancing enthusiastically. The rawboned guy who'd been doing the hearty laughing was dancing the most enthusiastically of all with a chubby peroxide blonde right next to us, me and the archivist's woman. It seemed like he bumped into me every half-minute and, each time, excused himself with a big old lopsided grin.

The fourth number was a slow one, "Whiskey Trip," and she wanted to dance again. I started to but on the first bars, Gary begins to lament: ". . . I can almost see us now in Acapulco"—and the woman pushed herself into me. Well I know trouble when I feel it—and I told her we should sit this one out.

At the same time, the peroxide blonde was saying to her partner, "Darrell, you just about done wore me out! I'm gonna sit myself down."

She sounded like June Carter Cash on that San Quentin album when Johnny tells her, "I like to watch you talk." And her response is, "I'm talking with my mouth!"

"Okay, darlin!" exclaimed the laugher. And turning towards me—having noticed my partner walk away—he said, "I been bumping into you so much, it's like we's acquainted. Why'd'nt you come over, let me buy you an alcoholic beverage."

I went over and let him buy me one and some more after that; then I bought a couple of rounds, and then it was his turn again. Meanwhile, other people came to the table and went away. The peroxide blonde, Darlene, was one who stayed, as did a girlfriend of hers.

After a solid hour of drinking, Darrell turned to his girl, "Darlin . . ." (at least that's the way it sounded, maybe he was just calling her by name) "Darlin, you must be plenty rested now. How 'bout I play some more Gary?"

She was all for it. Darrell punched in the other ten Gary Stewart sides on the box, as well as the eight he'd played before, and we all got out on the floor. My partner was Gina. She worked in a restaurant, cooking seafood, but it was only temporary, she assured me, until she could find work at her profession, which was as a beautician. But her real dream in life was to open a shop that sold false eyelashes and false nails. She figured St. Augustine was ready for it.

All of that I heard in bits and pieces over the course of the five fast numbers. The sixth was a slow one. She didn't slam herself into me, like the other one had done, but she let me know her body was there and close.

"You married?" she asked.

"No, how about you?"

"Not for the last five years."

"Oh."

"You got yourself a girlfriend?"

"Not one of those either," and I was glad to be hearing myself saying it.

"You're not . . . uh . . . ?"

"Nope."

"Don't be offended now."

"I won't be."

"Aren't you going to ask me if I have a boyfriend?"

78

"No, I'm not."

"I sort of do, but it's a sort of on-and-off kind of thing. That doesn't scare you, does it?"

"No, but what do you think'll happen if he comes walking in here tonight?"

"He won't. He's in Gainesville, working. It's about over, I think."

She put her head on my shoulder and I thought she moved just a little bit closer.

"You're not lying, are you?" She lifted her head. "About having a girlfriend? So many fellows tell lies."

"I'll never lie to you, Gina."

"Oh, I like it when you say my name."

She closed whatever space was still between us and we danced until the owner started playing with the lights. He had already pulled the plug on the jukebox but half the couples stayed on the floor grinding away.

"Time to take it home, folks. You gonna be more comfortable doing it there. Come and get one for the road and then move on out."

Just about every bar in town would pour you a beer or a mixed drink in a plastic cup to take with you. The two drive-in liquor stores did the same thing.

As we were going out to the parking lot, Gina suggested we go back to her place, and there wasn't any argument. She and Darlene went in one car and Darrell and I followed in his white pickup truck. The women lived in a trailer park at Vilano Beach which was across the inlet and a mile from the Spanish Armada.

The trailer was an aluminum-sided one-bedroom in the sand dunes. Gina brought out beers and Darrell started

79

picking through the tapes. "Now, Jim—(Gee-yum)—y'all ever hear of Charlie Rich up there in Canada?"

"Well, I can't speak for everybody up there but I sure have."

"That's one sumbitch who can sure sing. Am I right?"

"You're not wrong."

So he put on Charlie Rich and we resumed where we'd left off at the Spanish Armada. The first song was "The Most Beautiful Girl in the World," and the Silver Fox wasn't more than half a minute into the second, "Every Time I Touch You I Get High," when Gina said, "Come on with me, honey bunch."

She took me by the hand to the bedroom and when we came out an hour later, still holding hands, Darrell was lying on the couch with a beer balanced on his belly and three cans near him on the floor. Darlene was asleep in a recliner with her chin on her chest. Charlie Rich had finished singing.

Darrell held the beer with one hand and shook the index finger of the other. "I hope you two didn't do anything naughty in there."

"We did," Gina said. "And maybe some night soon we're gonna do something naughty in here, too."

"Well it's been awfully quiet out here," Darrell said. "Too quiet. I guess I'll head on home."

"Yeah, me too," I said.

Darrell asked me how I planned on getting there and I told him I'd walk. He said he'd drive me.

"Hell, you will," Gina told him. "You want to drive yourself the shape you're in that's bad enough but you're not driving this man. I just got him."

He sobbed some more and I said I'd see him later.

Darrell got up with tears in his eyes.

"Wait. Don't go for another minute. I'm so embarrassed you got to give me a chance to explain."

"You don't owe me any explanation, man. That's all right. It's just that it's late and I got to walk home."

While I was talking, I was looking at him and the tears were just streaming down his face.

He sniffed.

"I know you're supposed to get over these things but I never did. And now she's dead."

"Oh, man. You were going with her and she died?"

"No. She lied to me, cheated on me, stole from me, and finally threw my ass out but that didn't stop me from loving her. I loved her and loved her and she wouldn't have anything to do with me, but I still deep down thought that something would happen and we would get back together. And then two years ago she up and got killed on me. Auto wreck."

I told him how sorry I was and he blew his nose and wiped at his eyes, and I reached for the doorknob.

"Wait just one more minute, Gee-yum."

He went to a closet and moved some clothes off a box that was handmade out of plywood. He lifted the lid, reached inside and came up with a sheet and a pillow.

"Thanks, Darrell, but I got to head back to my own place."

"No, no. You don't understand."

He put the pillow against his face and closed his eyes.

"The smell's almost gone. I can't hardly smell her any more."

He began to cry again, and I began to leave again. But when he looked at me, his expression was so tortured and helpless that I couldn't keep going.

"When she threw me out for the last time, I knew it was the last time. She said, 'I'll give you one half-hour to pack up and be gone. If I get back here and you're still here, I get the law.' So I gathered up my stuff and loaded it into the truck and came back for a last look around and I looked at the sheets on the bed, the way they were all wrinkled up, and it was her made the wrinkles 'cause I'd been sleeping on the couch for weeks—and I just grabbed them off the bed. And the pillow. This same pillow, these same sheets."

He was standing there in the middle of his cottage, sheets spilling out of his arms, looking like a pitiful overgrown baby who didn't have a teddy bear.

"I ain't been much use ever since. Much use to women, that is. I do my regular work all right but I ain't much for the romantic work. Sometimes I can get it done but like Darlene over there says, 'Darrell, you're just not reliable. I don't want to get hotted up for nothing.' So Gee-yum, what you see before you this evening or morning is one sorrowful son-of-a-bitch."

I left him weeping into his pillow and patterned sheets, and headed back for my first sleep in the trailer. The oak trees dripped Spanish moss, there was no breeze to stir the palm fronds. I could hear the faint groan of motors gearing down for traffic lights on Highway Number One.

At nine in the morning, about five hours later, there was a knock on my door. It was Darrell, all scrubbed and combed, with a sheepish expression but no hangover. He said good morning then looked down at his shoes. They were brown, steel-toed lace-ups.

"I owe you an apology."

"You got nothing to apologize for. Come on in for a cup of coffee."

I made the coffee while he sat quietly at the table. When I set the cup down in front of him, he said. "Uh, you know, all that stuff I was going on about last night?"

"Yeah."

"Well don't believe none of it, all right?"

"If you say so."

"No, I mean it now. What I said about the sheets and pillows and especially what I told you about being unreliable around the women. Hell, I always get the job done. You better believe it. It's just that I got a lively imagination when I've been drinking. Not a word of truth in it. I don't know why but I say the same things every time. Yessir, just start crying and give out the same old sob story. So forget it, hear?"

"I will."

"All right, then. Say, how about we go up to the highway, that place there and get some breakfast."

"Sounds good."

"I'm buying."

"Sounds better."

We finished the coffee and left the trailer.

"I bet you don't like grits," Darrell said.

"I bet I do."

"How about chitlins?"

"You gotta be kidding."

"They're good eatin, Gee-yum."

THE MUG

"Jesus, Sylvester, this glass you give me is filthy. Don't you never wash your goddamned dishes, or what?"

"What're you busting my balls for? You don't like the way it is at my house you can go somewhere else, eh?"

"Did I just hear you call this dump your house? What you mean is your dinky skid row room."

"Whatever."

"And if you don't like what I'm saying, I can always go home."

"All right. Calm down, Horace, don't get your knickers in a knot."

"Oh, yeah. He's acting real friendly now. Couldn't be because I'm the one that brought the booze."

"No, it's 'cause I'm generally a good-natured individual. There's always another bottle to be had."

"Yeah, and where the fuck is it? Where's the guy with the bottle? When did you call him? What, half an hour ago?"

"Fifteen minutes."

"He better get here quick. We're almost finished this one."

"Are you ever in a bad mood there, Horace."

"Yeah, you know, I'm sorry. It's these heart palpitations, they're getting worse. Not only that but I got the colitis. So I have diarrhea three or four times a day. It's hell getting old."

"Tell me about it."

"You're just a young fuck, Sylvester, me lad."

"You mean I haven't had a fuck since I was young. I'm seventy-four fucking years old."

"S'what I mean. Compared to me you're young."

"What're you seventy-seven, seventy-eight?"

"Seventy-eight. And you, you got nothing wrong with you."

"Hell, I don't. My back hurts nearly all the time. That's why I don't wash the dishes so good. Hurts like hell leaning forward over the sink."

"That's nothing."

"Nothing? Yeah, well. Shit, the bad thing is I don't have any money. You got more than me."

"Well, it ain't like I'm rich."

"You don't live in a fucking little room. You got a nice apartment."

"Veteran's building. Sure I don't pay much rent but I don't have much left over."

"Well, all's I got is the pension. I got to pick up cans on the street to make it 'til the first of the month."

"Why don't you pick up bottles? You get twice as much money."

"Yeah but they're too heavy. I mean, ten bottles weigh more than twice as much as twenty cans. And with my fucked-up back I have a hard enough time lugging the sack around as it is."

88

There was a knock on the door.

"Must be our man."

Sylvester groaned as he started to lift himself out of the chair.

"Ah, shit. I'm having a spasm."

Horace looked at him. There was another knock.

"Whyn't you move your fat ass over to the door?"

Horace let the cab driver in. He was a young guy that they'd never seen before. He set the bottle of rye down on top of the two-burner hot plate. Sylvester gave Horace his share of the money. Horace handed it over to the cab driver, told him 'See you,' and reached for the door.

"Hey, give the kid a drink. You want a drink, kid?"

"Well, I don't know."

He was probably thirty. Curly-headed kid, looked pleasant enough, not like a punk.

"Freddy always has a drink with us," Sylvester said. "Where's he at?"

"He had a stroke."

"Oh, geez," Sylvester said.

"Too bad," Horace said. "The poor fuck."

"Hey, kid. Grab a glass from the cabinet over the hot plate. Pour yourself one."

The kid found a glass and looked at it closely, said, "Uh, this . . ."

"Yeah, I know what you mean." Horace looked at the cab driver, nodded toward Sylvester. "Says he can't clean up too good on account of his back hurts."

"That's right," Sylvester said. "Wash it at the sink, kid. And crack open the bottle."

"Why the hell don't you let the man use your expensive

antique French drinking mug you got over there in your closet?" Horace asked.

"German."

The driver poured them each a drink then put a couple of inches in his own glass.

"I mean, you got filthy pots and plates and filthy glasses, and then you got this one old mug that don't have a speck of dust on it because you keep it wrapped up in paper and in a box."

"I can't let nobody use it because it might break. You don't ever see me use it, do you?"

"You treat it like a holy fucking relic."

"It is kind of like a holy relic. The monks made these mugs for themselves. They didn't make many of them because there weren't many monks. And it was the tradition that . . ."

"Yeah, yeah. I've heard it all a thousand times. You and your fancy antique mug."

"Excuse me," said the cab driver, looking at Horace then at Sylvester. "But, uh, I wouldn't mind hearing the story. I'm kind of interested in old stuff."

Sylvester gave him an appreciative nod. "It's old, all right. Must be five hundred years old."

"Yeah, sure," Horace smirked. "And the stupid looking thing has been handed down from hand to hand in the family for all these centuries ever since your great-great—I don't know how many greats—great-grandfather decided he didn't want to be a monk anymore on account of he was chasing some Bavarian pussy."

"This monk in my family," Sylvester told the cab driver, "he fell in love with one of the girls that used to come to the monastery gate to get the brandy that the monks made. So he left the Order to marry her."

"That's an interesting story," the cab driver said.

"It is?" Horace said. "Fuck's so interesting about it?" They both ignored him.

"Would you like to take a look at it?"

"Oh, yeah. I sure would."

"Christ, kid," Horace said. "He must like you. I've known him ten years and heard the story six hundred times and I've only seen the damn thing twice."

Sylvester took his time getting up but he didn't groan doing it.

"You forgot to complain about your back," Horace said, but he didn't get any response.

The closet was no more than six feet from where Sylvester was sitting. The whole room was only twelve feet by fifteen. There wasn't a door to the closet but, rather, a curtain on a rod. Sylvester pushed the curtain aside and lifted a box down from the high shelf. It was a cardboard box like you'd get to protect your purchase at a department store. The old man took the box and placed it on top of the hot plate so it was at his chest level and he didn't have to lean forward. He took the lid off, revealing tissue paper and chips of polystyrene that had a faint blue tinge to them.

The cab driver was watching attentively. Horace sat in his chair, knocking back rye. He glanced over, said, "See them plastic things. They kind of remind me of Cheezits. Hey, Sylvester, you got any Cheezits around here. Anything to eat?"

The two men ignored him. They were looking at the mug sitting there in its cradle.

91

"I thought it would be bigger," said the cab driver.

"Well, it was used for brandy which is why it has that shape. I forget what they call it."

"A balloon," said the driver. "Like you'd get a balloon of brandy."

"Oh, so you know a lot about antiques."

"Not all that much, but I'm interested in stuff that has to do with drinking."

"Yeah, me too," Horace called from his chair.

"It may not be big like a beer mug," Sylvester said, "but that don't mean it's not valuable."

"That's right. It is beautiful. I never saw a beer mug that was anywhere near as beautiful. That blue paint looks original. That's amazing. And those light marks here and there, I bet they were once white. Maybe they were marks of the cross. The trim around the lip, that looks like real gold leaf."

"I never knew what those two little loops were for," Sylvester said. "Do you know what they're for?"

"I think what they're for is, you hold the mug in your hand like you do with a modern brandy glass, you know, to keep the brandy warm. That's why your mug and modern glasses all have that balloon shape. Anyway, you could hold the mug in your hands or just one hand and put your fingers or just one finger through the loop. That way you keep it warm and it's not awkward to hold."

"It's amazing that you know all that stuff."

The cab driver shrugged. "Is there a mark on the underside of the mug?"

"Yeah, there's something under there."

Sylvester turned it upside down and the kid muttered, "Oh, wow."

"Yeah, that mean something?"

"If you ever see china or stoneware—any kind of factory-made pottery—it always has the maker's mark somewhere on it. You know, like a modern logo. But this isn't a manufacturer's mark. I mean, it's individual. You have that—what looks like two sides of a triangle, and it's over the crude cross. I'm guessing, but I'd say the triangle represents a church or a monastery that's protecting the cross, with everything that means. So each one of these that was made would have had a different mark and there couldn't have been many of them made, otherwise they would have had some sort of stamp in order to save them all the trouble."

Sylvester gently laid the mug onto its bed of plastic and paper.

"Do you think," he looked at the kid and his tongue darted over his lips. "Do you think it's worth much money?"

Horace looked over at them again.

"Yeah, I do."

Horace came over carrying his drink.

They both stared at the kid but the kid didn't say anything. He was looking at the mug.

"So, uh, how much do you think it might be worth?" Sylvester asked him.

"Yeah, how much?" Horace said.

"Well, I'm not an expert."

"Yeah, yeah. How much?" Horace said.

"I'd say, uh, conservatively speaking," the kid had his eyes fixed on the mug. "It has to be worth twenty, twenty-five."

"Fuck," said Horace. "Twenty, twenty-five fucking dollars!

Big fucking deal." He turned to Sylvester. "You and your god-damned precious antique mug. Jesus H. Christ."

Sylvester stared at the mug. He looked like he was going to cry.

"Thousand," said the kid. "Twenty, twenty-five thousand dollars. And I'd say that's a conservative estimate."

"Jesus," Horace muttered.

Sylvester still looked like he was going to cry. "I have to sit down."

He filled his glass and went to his chair.

"I could move into a better place. Get therapy for my back. I could . . . "

The old man shook his head slowly and his eyes filled with tears.

"Fuck you crying for?" Horace asked him. "You should be up dancing a jig or something. Or buy us another bottle, Mister Money-Bags. This one's almost dead."

"It just so happens I have another bottle in the cab. I was supposed to deliver it to another guy but he's probably passed out by now."

"Well, what're you waiting for?" Horace said. "Go get it."

The cab driver left. Sylvester kept staring off into space.

"Let me take a closer look at that damn mug," Horace said, and reached for it.

"Don't touch it!" Sylvester shouted. He pushed his hands down on the arms of his chair and groaned, trying to raise himself. Horace picked the mug up and held it over his head to look at the mark on the bottom.

"You son-of-a-bitch!" Sylvester was standing now and coming toward Horace. He got a hand on his arm and Horace spun around, still holding the mug aloft.

"It's not yours. Let go of it."

The door to the room opened.

Sylvester was coming at Horace who backed into the stand that held the hot plate.

"My fucking ankle," he said, and just as he was about to fall, the kid was there, and snatched the mug out of his hand. The kid took a nimble step to the side and Horace went down.

"Oh, shit. I think I sprained it."

Sylvester was out of breath, trying to talk. Finally he managed to say, "Gee kid, you saved my ass. I don't know how to thank you."

"You could let me have another drink."

"Sure thing, anything you want."

"I need one too," Horace said, "so I don't feel my ankle."

"The hell with him," Sylvester said to the cab driver, jerking his thumb at Horace. "Sit down here and tell me how you come to know so much about this kind of thing and how do I go about selling the mug."

The cab driver thought about how he liked the old man. In a few minutes Horace had begun to snore, flat out on the floor. The kid told Sylvester that ever since he was a boy he had been interested in old things and the stories behind them.

Sylvester listened to him but he was getting sleepy. In half an hour, Sylvester appeared to be sound asleep, his head back on the chair. The kid kept addressing him but the old man didn't answer. After a few more minutes of this, the kid got up and opened the door to the room. Then he came back and took the mug out of its box. He went to the door again and looked back at the old man sleeping with his mouth open. Yeah, he thought as he left the room, I like the old dude but I don't like him that much.

Six Dead, Nine Wounded

Larry, Dean and Chucky lugged plastic-wrapped sections of dressed moose to the rented cold storage locker, breathing heavily with the effort but still cracking jokes. Three trips it took from Chucky's van.

"Well, that's about got her. Hey, it was a damned good opening weekend," Dean said.

"Yeah, can't wait for that first steak," Larry said. "Well, I got to rock and roll, see you guys later. We on for rugby, Dean? Chucky, I'm sorry you can't make it anymore."

"Me too," Chucky said.

"I'm on," Dean said, getting into his car. "Next Saturday then."

They got into their vehicles and left.

Chucky Harper went home, pulled the van into its place in the underground lot at False Creek. He got out, opened the rear doors of the van. The plastic tarp was still on the floor but there wasn't much blood on it. He grabbed the

duffel and the gun bag, feeling the .303 through the
padded leather. Thought of the moose fixed there in the
sights. Chucky saw himself, exhaling gently before
squeezing the trigger. He smiled, or at least in his head he
smiled. It was a special moment, Chucky knowing it was
a perfect shot, the moose taking a couple of steps before
crashing. A few minutes later, Larry and Dean clapping
him on the back, kidding with him.

But heading for the elevator, his attention turned to
what awaited. Ellen starting on him the moment he
walked in. Tossing the word "macho" around. No surprise
there. She'd get on him about being with his buddies,
doing macho things like not shaving for three days. Bet it
makes you feel like a real man to kill a harmless animal. A
real man playing rugby in your shorts with all the other
real men. It's all repressed homosexuality, although you
don't realize it. Grabbing each other all the time. Her saying all that. The kids watching as she put him through the
wringer. His daughter staring at him with distaste. That
had been going on for two years now, since Ginny'd
turned eleven. Two years, not long after Ellen herself had
begun to change. Ginny used to like her daddy before
that. Marty, well, he was just confused. Didn't know what
to think about his father. Marty seemed to like him well
enough when they were alone together.

Chucky pressed the button for the fourth floor and the
elevator whined. I mean, Chucky thought, it's not as if we
have a tough life. Own a three-bedroom condo, both have
good jobs, kids aren't on drugs.

Looking back on it the next morning, Chucky would tell
himself he knew something was wrong even before he

98

opened the door. Knew somehow as he was putting the key into the lock. That frozen moment. Just like with the moose.

Still, even though he might have known before opening the door, when he did open it, and saw that the place was practically empty, he couldn't figure out what was going on. As if—what's the expression Ginny used? *What's wrong with this picture?*

What's wrong, dummy, is that all the furniture in the living room has been removed, except for your reclining chair and a radio that looks pretty forlorn sitting on the floor, on the wall to wall carpet, cord stretched to the socket that had been unseen for years, ever since the black leather sofa had been put in place.

The dining room table was gone, and all four chairs. There was a pale rectangle on the beige wall where the framed print of a native Indian mask had been. Well, he wouldn't miss that, Chucky caught himself thinking. In the kitchen, the counters were bare except for an electric kettle. He opened the cabinets and the drawers and found a tea towel, a dish, a mug, a bowl, one spoon, one fork, a paring knife and a can opener. Two cans of beer, the only things in the fridge. No food anywhere. There was half a bottle of dark rum and a couple of inches of schnapps in one of the cabinets.

Chucky had a hit from the bottle of rum before going to face the bedroom. The kids' rooms were empty. In their room, his and Ellen's—what used to be their room—only his things were hanging in the closet. His socks, under-wear and T-shirts, in a pile at the bottom of the closet. A couple of bags with his rugby gear in a corner of the room.

Where the bed used to be was a pillow, a sheet, and a sleeping bag. Chucky grabbed these and took them into the living room, thinking of the kid in the cartoon, who dragged his blanket everywhere.

Chucky poured rum into the mug and took it to his reclining chair. Ellen used to complain about the stain left on the back of the chair by the back of his head. Chucky had made the mistake of telling her that since he didn't use anything on his hair, and she used the thick, sticky gel—ever since she got that dyke haircut—that she got the back of her own trendy goddamned chair even dirtier, but at least he could wipe the back of his leather chair clean. That got her angry, the implication of it, but she had a comeback, saying, "As if you'd ever do anything like that. Wipe a chair or any fucking thing else. Any housework. You're too macho."

Saying that last line in the mocking tone she'd gotten so proficient at the last couple of years.

After he was in the chair a few minutes and had knocked back a couple ounces of rum, Chucky felt like he was snapping out of it. He'd been in a sort of daze since entering the place. Ellen was gone, her and the kids. She meant to stay gone, too. If it were temporary, she wouldn't have cleaned the place out. She must have been thinking and planning her escape for a long time. Probably was on the phone to the moving company the minute he'd closed the door on Friday night. He pictured them arriving at seven on Saturday morning. Two or three guys. They must have realized that they were leaving all the things that belonged to the man of the house. Did they picture the same thing happening to themselves?

100

Chucky thought back to meeting Ellen for the first time. At the motorcycle races. She was a different woman then, for sure. He had reminded her, not too long ago, of how different she had been. "Yeah, I hadn't woken up yet," she'd practically spit it at him, as if it was his fault she hadn't been what she called "liberated."

He could chart the changes in her. First, it was courses at night school. "Self-Actualization: Keeping in Touch with the Real You" was one of them. Then the changes in appearance coinciding with the courses and workshops. She stopped wearing make-up, a radical change for a girl who used to spend hours getting ready to go out. A year or so after that first course, Ellen had even stopped wearing deodorant. She didn't shave her legs or her underarms. Couldn't a woman be liberated, Chucky wondered, without being hairy and smelling bad?

Ellen had said something about how if a woman worried about her personal appearance she was only helping to perpetuate the female stereotype. Naturally, they had stopped having sex. Ellen had accused him of raping her. This was before he was aware they had stopped having sex. He had cuddled up to her back one morning and slipped it in, same as he'd done a hundred times before. "Rape!" she hollered. "Help!"

Chucky was angry now as he finished the rum in his mug and poured more. He conjured up a few dozen more bad memories and called her all sorts of names. And then he began to think about the kids. He staggered into their rooms and all at once he was sobbing. Then he got into the schnapps and got back into the goddamned E-Z Boy recliner and cried right out. Bawled like a baby. Some macho man.

He woke at seven on Monday morning and didn't know where the hell he was. His head throbbed like the engine in an old Norton he'd had when he was a kid. For at least thirty seconds, Chucky couldn't figure out what he was doing in a sleeping bag on the living room floor. When he figured it out, he felt like his life was empty and the world was meaningless.

He got to his feet. It was raining outside. He had a job to go to. Fancy that. Your world falls apart and so what? You still have to go to work and sell motorcycles. Maybe he ought to listen to his own sales pitch, the company's sales pitch. Get on the bike, torque her up and take off. Live Free.

Sorry to leave you people with all the extra work to do but I'm going to hit the open road, head into the unknown on my 1500cc Explorer.

Well, he couldn't do that. He wasn't a salesman anyway. He was the sales manager. Had worked his way up from mechanic, from fixing bikes in his dad's garage. Riding them around the neighbourhood when he was twelve. He was a thoroughly different breed of cat from what his son was.

Chucky, holding his razor, stared in the bathroom mirror at his hungover face. Thought about not shaving, about Ellen smirking, then realized he didn't have to be concerned with what she thought, and put down the razor. He got under the shower, turned the water as hot as he could stand it. Nice of her not to take the lump of pink soap from the ledge of the tub. He stayed under the water for several minutes, then dried off, got dressed and out of the place. She hadn't left him any coffee or anything to eat.

He lived in False Creek, less than a ten-minute walk to the motorcycle dealership. Chucky went into the café across the street, and Agnes had the coffee poured before he could sit down. "How you doing, Chucky?"

"All right. You?"

"I been better. I been worse."

"Yeah."

He ordered, drank coffee. Thought about telling her exactly how it was going. Like, So Agnes, I get in last night. No wife, no kids. Place was empty.

What would she say, You want a refill?

No, I want my life back. Wait. Do I really want my life back?

Chucky started working on the omelet. His head wasn't too bad now. What am I supposed to do, just take this shit? he wondered. Bitch turns my whole life upside down, doesn't even leave a note. If only Ellen had left a note on the back of an envelope: So long, dickhead. At least, that would have been personal. This, this way just showed contempt.

"You don't look like a happy camper, Chucky."

Agnes poured more coffee.

"I'm not."

"Troubles at home, eh?"

"You might say that, yeah."

"Too bad."

He bet Agnes wasn't the type to take self-actuality workshops. She was a good woman, worked hard, on her feet all day, didn't complain constantly. He knew that she lived on her own. Agnes was liberated, only nobody had told her she had to hit the world over the head with it.

103

When he got behind his desk, Chucky telephoned Group Gaia where Ellen worked. This was a business that linked women, via the Internet, to other businesses that catered only to women. They told him Ellen wasn't in. When Chucky asked if she had called in, he was brusquely informed that they didn't give out such information. He said he was her husband and the woman repeated that they didn't give out such information.

Chucky telephoned Ellen's parents, asked them if they'd heard from her.

"Why?" the mother asked. "You two fighting again?"

Chucky told her what had happened.

"What did you do to her, Charles?"

"Listen, just tell me if you've heard from her."

The woman began advising him as to what he could do to be a better husband. The father was on the extension. He could hear the guy breathing. Finally, the old man got up the nerve to speak. "She's not here. We haven't talked to her for over a week."

"Frank!"

"See you."

He stared at the papers on his desk while trying to figure out what to do next. Ellen's best friend worked at a women's shelter, but he knew they didn't take calls from men. Hell, even if he telephoned the woman at home she wouldn't tell him anything. He didn't know the names of Ellen's other friends. Ellen went on and on about her friends, how they'd overcome such terrible circumstances and emerged "whole." They were goddesses, she'd said. But to Chucky they all sounded the same, one goddess without a name.

So he did his work, took care of business. Chucky kept expecting the phone to ring and Ellen to be on the other end; he half-hoped she'd call, half-dreaded she'd call.

But she didn't call and there were no messages when he got back to the condo. Hell, she had taken the answering machine. He thought about her voice on the machine. Cool and noncommittal, as if she hadn't wanted to take a chance on showing any hint of warmth in case it might be a man calling.

He went to the Granville Market for groceries, and found himself searching the crowd for her, for the kids. Then he felt like an idiot for doing so. As if she would be in the vicinity. For all Chucky knew, she might have gone to Toronto or California. It was the not knowing that bothered him. Then, as he turned oranges over in his hand, it occurred to Chucky that he might call the police. She had, after all, kidnapped their children. But he should wait a couple of days before seriously considering that. Also, he had to try and figure out what was going on in her mind. Ellen had to assume he'd call the cops and, therefore, she'd have some story ready. He remembered a couple of months ago, her smirking at him, saying, "You men are so naïve. We women are always two steps ahead of you at any given time."

Three days passed and during that time Chucky was usually either angry or feeling sorry for himself. There were also those rare moments when he got wildly excited, picturing himself as a footloose single man. But he couldn't face going out on the town, sitting alone at a movie or in a bar by himself. So he bought a television and a VCR— naturally, Ellen had taken the others—and rented movies.

It was on the fifth night that he watched an old one with Alan Ladd as a private eye. Him in his trench coat, hat pulled down over his eyes, talking tough and witty at the same time.

And watching that movie gave Chucky the idea of calling a private eye. Hell, why not? What was he supposed to do, just sit there? What if someone asked him, "Your wife took the kids and vanished, cleaned out the joint, so what did you do about it?"—"Uh, nothing."—"Nothing?"—"Yeah, I didn't do a damn thing."

Chucky got out the Yellow Pages. The first four companies he called weren't into that kind of thing. They only did electronic stuff. Surveillance. Corporate security. You could hire a person to drive to the parking lot of your business competitor and listen in on what was going on in the boardroom or the president's office. They were insulted when Chucky mentioned he had a missing persons case.

The fifth place was called Allied Information Services and after Chucky explained the situation, the man who answered the phone said they ought to meet in person. Chucky sort of wanted to go to the guy's office—he knew he was being foolish—check it out, maybe he had a slinky secretary, but the guy wanted to come see the condo. Chucky didn't understand why, but he said okay.

The private eye's name was Harvey Fryberg, and he was taller than Alan Ladd, dressed in a blue nylon windbreaker and wearing white running shoes. When he took off the windbreaker, Chucky saw the guy was thick around the middle. The only clue he was a private eye, the way Chucky thought about it, was the way he scoped the rooms of the apartment, but then again Fryberg might have been an interior decorator. He had a heavy face, thinning curly black hair. The guy was smart though, caught Chucky checking him out, said, "I'm the kind of guy that doesn't stand out in a crowd. You do what I do for a living that's the way you should look."

He asked Chucky for photographs. Chucky had ones of the kids, but not of Ellen. The guy took notes as Chucky described Ellen, asked about credit cards and bank accounts. Fryberg told him he would find Ellen and the kids and convey any message Chucky wanted to give as long as it was non-threatening, but he couldn't bring them back, do anything illegal. Chucky said that was fine and asked how much it would cost. Fryberg told him and Chucky agreed. Fryberg said it might take a couple of days, three maybe, because tomorrow was Sunday. When the guy left, Chucky wondered how he could do it in only a few days.

But, damn if the guy didn't call on Tuesday afternoon. "Well, I found them," he said.

"Christ."

"But I have to add on something for expenses. The cops hassled me and I missed the last ferry back, had to stay over."

"Where, where for chrissakes?"

"They're on the Sunshine Coast. You know where that is?"

"On the Island, right?"

"No, it's just over the mountains from Squamish, but there's no road over the mountains so you have to take the ferry from Horseshoe Bay in West Van."

"Yeah, why are they there? What're they doing? Ellen got another guy?"

"It's not another guy she's got."

"You mean . . . ?"

"Yeah, well, this . . . this woman . . . is definitely the romantic interest. I sat next to them in a restaurant one morning, at the next table, drinking coffee, pretending to read the local rag and listened to them gab away. These are two serious man-haters. And it's a wonder your ears weren't ringing, as my granny used to say. Anyway, you come over here and confront this woman that your wife is cozy with, well, you better be ready to tangle. She's a tough broad. Runs a school and your kids are now enrolled in that school."

"Ginny and Marty?"

"Maybe that's what they used to be but now they're Moonstone and Asgaya."

"Moonstone and Asgaya?"

"Yeah, Moonstone, you know, that's not too bad but you want to know what Asgaya means?"

"No, but tell me anyway."

"Asgaya is a character from Cherokee Indian mythology who, uh, went both ways."

"What?"

"You know, a bi-sexual kind of thing."

Chucky was silent.

"It gets worse," Fryberg said.

"It does?"

"Oh, yeah. This dyke runs the school, like I said. And at this school, half of the week, the boys dress as girls and the girls dress as boys, which isn't all that big a change for the girls because most of the girls and women over here— that's the way they dress anyway. This is all happening in a place called Roberts Creek, midway between Gibsons and Sechelt."

"So my Marty goes to school in a dress?"

"Asgaya, yeah. Three days one week, two days the next. The theory behind this is that the kids 'won't be forced into stereotypical sexual roles and are free to explore both sides of their nature, the feminine and masculine side.' I'm quoting the brochure."

"How do the kids seem to be doing?"

"In my opinion—and I'm no psychologist, you understand . . . in my opinion, they are not happy campers. The boy especially."

"This other woman, the girlfriend or boyfriend, whatever the fuck she is, she stay over?"

"Uh huh. They neck in front of the kids. I'm walking down the road, just happen to be passing by their place, you know what I mean, and the two of them are sitting on the steps and this other woman is macking her like a horny high school boy. Dyke comes up for air, sees me, gives me the finger, goes right back to it. Then they went inside, the dyke's hand on your wife's rear end, and . . . "

"Okay, okay."

"Anyway, I'm in the general store. They call it a general store but what it really is, it's a store where they sell things at double the price you'd pay for them at the supermarket. You go in there you can get a copy of *Wooden Boat* or a wilted head of organic lettuce, maybe a little crystal—I don't mean meth—for your window sill. They got a bulletin board where all the shamans and healers advertise. They got a big poster for something coming up next Saturday called the Meeting of the Clans. Only it ain't the

Macdonalds and the Campbells, it's the hippies and the Indians. Excuse me, I mean, the native persons, and the clan of the unwed lesbians of colour with disabilities, for all I know. So I walk out of there with my ice cream cone and there's a Mountie in his car, and he gets out, ID's me. Wants to know what I'm doing; says they got a report describing me, people said I was lurking."

"What did you tell him?"

"Said I was minding my own business, eating an ice cream cone, heading down to the pier to enjoy the scenery. Told him I like it over here, thinking of buying property."

"You tell him what you were working on?"

"No way. Things are strictly confidential with me. Don't worry about that."

"Did he take you in?"

"No but he detained me long enough for me to miss the last ferry. Stayed at some place in Gibsons called the Irwin Motel. I'll send you the receipt with my report."

"Uh, listen. Fryberg."

"Yeah?"

"Did you, uh, did you see my kid, my boy, in a dress?"

"Yeah, I'm afraid so. Walking to school. But he was with some other boys and they were in dresses too. Those boys, they looked fucking miserable."

The next three days, Chucky went to work, worked, came home, sat in his chair and thought about everything. Agnes at the restaurant asked him what was bothering him; he said, Oh, you know. They asked him at work and he said nothing was bothering him. He sat in the E-Z Boy and went over it in his mind, tossing the ball up and down,

110

the one signed by each and every one of the All-Blacks. He thought about being on the field, running with the ball or running after the guy who had the ball. Thought of being in the bush, going after the moose, the bear, whatever. Thought of being a Man; thought of Ellen being inside his mind, making fun of him for thinking like that. Okay, he changed it to being a real Person. Someone who didn't just let things happen to him, didn't let others control his life. "It's one thing to allow someone to screw up my life. I mean, that's bad enough," Chucky thought he was saying it to himself, but realized he was talking out loud. "But it's another thing to let her screw up the lives of my kids. And me just sitting here letting her do it."

He was about to throw the ball at the pale rectangle on the wall where the print of the mask had been but he was too much aware of himself, wouldn't get any satisfaction out of it because he was standing back watching himself. That's the feeling he wanted, same way he felt having that moose in his sights, standing back, taking a breath, exhaling. Master of the situation.

There was a Tourism Information counter on the ferry. Chucky picked up a map of the Sunshine Coast, but the lady told him he didn't need it to get to Roberts Creek. Just follow the highway, turn left on Roberts Creek Road, go down toward the water. There were just a few shops, a general store and a place called The Wellington Boot Café, known locally as The Welly. "Yes, that's Creeker central," the lady said, and Chucky thought she kind of pressed her lips together with distaste.

"I've heard a lot about the, uh, the Creek," Chucky said. "What kind of people live there?"

"Lots of what used to be known as hippies. Only now they're middle-aged and older. They have these houses down there that I sure as shootin' couldn't afford. You'll see a man with long grey hair and a bald spot. That kind. New Agers I guess you'd call them."

Chucky wondered if it was a bad idea to talk to her but decided he didn't care. The lady told him it was a big weekend for the Creekers, weekend of the annual Meeting of the Clans. Same thing Fryberg had mentioned.

Something else Chucky wondered about was the van. Maybe it would look too suspicious. Maybe Ellen would notice it. Maybe the kids would recognize it. But, on the other hand, he was beyond caring.

The first word that came to Chucky's mind when he got to Roberts Creek was "quaint." Cottages by the side of the road and big estates, according to the real estate listings, down driveways that seemed to disappear into the forest. Saabs and Volvos and SUV's out front of the general store had bumper stickers with slogans that made Chucky want to throw up or punch the owner. The people he saw wandering about all had the bland middle-class superior look.

Chucky stayed in the van, checking everything out. He was sitting there across the street from The Welly when he saw Ellen and the kids. Jesus. He ducked his head. He had been parked next door to the house that they came out of. Them and Ellen's lover.

Chucky peeked over the dashboard. She looked like a stumpy truck driver, some guy who used to lift weights but had given up and put on weight. The dyke was barking orders. Chucky saw her make a grab for Marty's arm, "Asgaya, you get over here."

Marty yanked his arm away from her. Good boy.

"Get back in the house and change your clothes."

Marty hung his head. Ellen said, "Do as you're told."

Marty turned around and headed for the house.

Chucky was surprised that he didn't have any feelings about Ellen. Didn't care that she was hip to hip with the dyke. Instead his attention was for Ginny. He felt like weeping, seeing his daughter's blank expression. Like a zombie. Go back to the house, Chucky said to her in his mind, stay with your brother. But she didn't, she kept walking across the road, eyes straight ahead.

There must have been a couple of hundred people heading for the café, or the grounds in back of the café. After a few minutes, Chucky heard drum beats, and then there was chanting. He thought of going to the house and getting Marty but, no, he had a plan and he was sticking to it.

Chucky waited for over an hour before the people started coming around to the front of the café, the side door of the van open six inches, the .303 on the floor. He turned on the ignition, went back between the two seats, knelt on the floor and picked up the .303.

He saw the dyke first, got her in the sights, exhaled and fired. Chucky watched her drop. People near her didn't even know she'd been shot, it was as if she'd fainted. Where the hell was Ellen? There she was a few yards behind, walking with Ginny. Then Ellen saw that something had happened and she walked ahead, breaking away from the girl. Good. Chucky fired again. Missed. Well, he missed Ellen. Hit some young guy. Got her with the second shot. Added another to make sure. Three down and still people didn't know what was happening. Well, what the fuck, Chucky thought, he had only been planning on bagging the two of them but since he'd already hit one extra, he might as well keep shooting. Why the hell not? These people were pathetic anyway. Had answers for all of society's ills but were too stupid to know they were being shot at. So he took time to choose his next three victims, picked faces that he particularly disliked, but then, after a few more moments, even these morons figured out what was happening so Chucky just sprayed the crowd. Man, those hippies, or whatever you'd call them, just dropped like they had too much weed in their paper.

Finally, Chucky slid the door closed and got behind the wheel. He saw a Lincoln SUV pull away from the general store and start in the direction of Sechelt. One bright spark across the road pointed at it and started hollering. Others looked at the SUV and ran after it. Nobody noticed Chucky as he drove off, turned left on the coast road. The tourist map said it would take him back to Gibsons. He wondered how long it would be before the Mounties nabbed him. If they were as dim as the hippies, he'd probably make it all the way to Gibsons.

He did make it back to Gibsons. If they were on the lookout for a white van, they weren't going to have to work at it, him sitting there in heavy traffic. Stop and go a few yards between malls and franchise restaurants on the highway. Plenty of time to think about stuff, sitting there like that, but he didn't really think about what he'd just done. It was like a movie he'd once seen. He'd walked away from the theatre and it was over.

Chucky saw two motels facing each other across the highway. One was the Irwin—Chucky remembered Fryberg saying he'd stayed there. "Well, I'll just wait there for the Mounties," he said to himself.

There was a wall clock in the office. Only three-thirty. "I'll put my bag in the room," he told the Korean guy, "and walk over to the mall."

"Good. Bag in room. Mall that way."

There were two beds in the room. Chucky took the one farthest from the door. Laying the rifle, in its case, on the other bed, he imagined the Mounties coming through the door. "The gun's right there, officer." Imagined the line in the newspaper, "The suspect offered no resistance when . . ."

Chucky went to the mall, a pretty dreary place, actually; dimly lit, same shops you'd see at any mall. There was a hair cutting place, one barber up front, half a dozen stylists toward the back. Chucky saw the barber had rugby posters around his mirrors. There was one old dude in the chair, another waiting. Chucky took a seat. He couldn't be accused of trying to avoid arrest, he'd told the Korean guy where he'd be, waiting peacefully in the barber shop. Twenty minutes later he was in the chair talking to the barber about rugby. The barber was about his age, a bit huskier, a bit less hair. "How do you want it?"

"Cut it real close."

"It's been a long time since you've had it cut, eh?"

"Yeah, I've, uh, been working in the bush."

"You want it short as mine?"

"Shorter if you can do it. And can you take off the beard and moustache?"

"My kind of guy."

115

"That's right," said Chucky. "So you play rugby?"

"Oh, every Saturday. We got a team over here. You?"

"Used to. But the wife put a stop to that. You know how it is."

"Yeah, but my wife doesn't care. Just bring home the money, drive the boys to soccer, girls to ballet."

"You're lucky." Yeah, Chucky thought. If Ellen were like that—had been like that—she'd still be alive.

The guy told him about his team, how they even had a clubhouse, a building they rented cheap from the town, had parties there, got together to drink beer after a game. Sounded pretty good.

Chucky told him about his trip five years ago to New Zealand to see the All-Blacks on their home turf. It was the barber's turn to tell him he was lucky.

When the haircut and shave were done, the barber asked him how long he was going to be in town and Chucky told him not very long. The guy said that's too bad, I would have enjoyed talking to you some more. Me too, Chucky said. That's the way it goes.

Chucky took a turn around the rest of the mall but there wasn't much to see. There was a liquor store and he went in to get some beer. He was going to get his usual high-test tall-boys but thought better of it. When the law busted down the door, he didn't want them thinking he had been under the influence. So he got a six-pack of goddamn Kokanee Light.

He went back to the motel, had a shower, watched television. He didn't want to go out to eat in case the Mounties showed, so he called to have a pizza delivered. He went to sleep at midnight, wondering what the hell the Mounties

SIX DEAD, NINE WOUNDED

were doing. You'd think, Chucky thought to himself, they would have figured it out by now. Certainly, they had a description of the van, they must have called the ferries and learned that he hadn't driven on the boat which meant the van had to be on the Coast somewhere. If he were a Mountie, he'd certainly make the rounds of the motels. The van was sitting out there pretty obvious in the light from the lamp over the motel room door.

Waking the next morning, Chucky didn't know where he was for a moment. Then he had an image from the day before, the people in his sights. It was like a bit from a movie, part of a trailer. "Chucky Goes Berserk." Was he berserk? He felt detached from what had happened. A psycho? If he was a psycho would he know it?

His next thought was that he wasn't in a cell at the local cop shop. He looked between the blinds and didn't see five guys in uniform out front of the motel room, guns aimed at his door.

He left the room, got in and started the van. The Korean guy was walking across the lot with a broom and a bucket. The man nodded.

"I left the key on the bed," Chucky called out the window and waved. ("He seemed like nice man not mass murderer," the motel owner said.)

There was a place just down the road called Robbie's Pancake House. Chucky was hungry; he felt pretty damned good, happy too. He went into the Pancake House and was being led to a table for one when someone called, "Hey!" Chucky looked up. It was the barber who was at a booth with two women.

Chucky nodded and the guy waved him over. "Hey, sit

with us. This is the wife, Pam, and her sister Debby. I'm Jack, by the way."

"Chucky Harper. Pleased to meet you."

The wife was a heavy-set pleasant woman; the sister was cute, in good shape, what you'd call perky. They were all headed for the city; the women were going shopping at Granville Island. Chucky's good mood suddenly got even better. These were real women. The barber was talking about rugby. He was trying to get a team organized for kids.

"I got a bunch of clothes and shoes from when I used to coach," Chucky heard himself saying. "You could have them for your kids, but I don't know how I'd get them to you."

"That would be great. Maybe you could bring them over on your next trip to the Coast or I could go in some time and get them."

"I don't think I'm coming over any time soon."

"Going away?"

"Yeah, for a while."

"Oh, well. Hey maybe I could come over to your place while the ladies are shopping."

"Jack!" his wife interrupting. "Don't impose on the man."

"Sorry, but . . ."

"Hey, it's all right." Chucky said. "I'll give you my address and you can stop by later."

"Or, Jack, you can hang out with the nice man," Debby said, flirting with him. "And you guys can meet us in a few hours and we'll go for drinks."

She winked at Chucky and he smiled. The sister elbowed her and they laughed. Chucky thinking it had

118

been over a year since he'd had sex. That would be good, very good. He'd have to stay unarrested for that. Hell, maybe he could get away with all this.

"You need a ride into town?" the barber asked.

"I rented a van. Gotta return it before I get on the ferry."

"Leave it in the lot. Just call them and they'll come and pick it up. That's the way they do it here in the boonies. We'll drive you in."

Chucky went to the counter, asked to use the phone, pretended to talk into it, the barber and the women watching him. He hung up. "It's all arranged. I'll get my stuff out of the van."

Chucky put the gun case in his duffel bag and walked across the lot, got in the back of the Honda Accord with Debby. They drove to the dock and onto the ferry, and by the time they reached Horseshoe Bay forty minutes later, they were fast friends. These were the kind of people Ellen wouldn't have had anything to do with unless it was to lecture the women.

They drove to Granville Island, dropping the women off, and then Chucky directed Jack the barber to the condo, and into the underground parking lot.

"Hey, my sister-in-law likes you," the barber said, as they got in the elevator. "She's on the lookout for a guy now. Split with her husband about six months ago. You're her type. She's always saying she likes 'manly' men."

They laughed about that, Chucky feeling good, saying, "And I like womanly women."

They pulled into a parking stall and killed the engine.

"I just broke up too—my wife and I," Chucky said, "so don't be shocked when you see how empty the place is. I let her have everything rather than arguing. Just about all I do have left in the apartment is the rugby gear."

The barber stood in the middle of the living room. He had a view into the kitchen, all three bedrooms. "Nothing sadder than an empty home."

"Yeah. You're right there. What can I get you to drink?"

"Beer's good."

It was when he was twisting off the tops of the bottles that Chucky got the idea. The barber talking, Chucky watching him, thinking the guy is my height, my age, with my short haircut we kind of look similar. Then he knew he was going to do it.

He handed the guy a beer, said, "Please, pull up a floor and have a seat."

The barber laughed but remained standing. Chucky told him to wait a minute and he went into his room, came back with four shopping bags filled with rugby stuff. There were team shorts and tops in one bag, a couple of balls, the rest of the stuff mostly posters and rugby magazines.

"Oh, man. The kids will love this."

"There's plenty more in my storage place. Enough stuff to outfit a team—two teams."

"Let me give you some money for all this."

"No, man. Don't mention it. I'm not using it and I'd be happy for you to have it."

"You're gonna make some kids happy."

"Then it's a good deal."

The barber finished the beer. Chucky asked him if he wanted to go get the stuff, and the barber said sure thing.

"I'll take the rest of the six-pack with us."

They got to the cold storage building and Chucky

directed the barber to the locker he rented with the guys. After Chucky opened it, the barber said, "What's that in there next to the gear?"

"Moose. Went hunting not too long ago. It's my third of the animal. Guess the gear ought to go in your trunk."

The barber opened the trunk and Chucky took out his duffel bag, unzipped it and brought out the rifle case.

"I didn't have so much luck with the wild animals on the Coast," he said. "This belongs to the guy in the office. I have to return it to him. I'll be right back."

"Okay, I'll load the stuff."

"Help yourself to another beer."

"Thanks."

Chucky jogged across the lot to the far side of the building, went around the corner. Took the gun out of the case, popped in the clip, adjusted the sight, and peeked around the building. The barber standing there, left arm up, hand gripping the edge of the raised trunk, right hand holding the can of beer. Him not looking in Chucky's direction.

Chucky got him in focus. Poor guy. Right arm going up, head going back, lip of the beer can just now touching his lips. Chucky fired, and the barber's head exploded. Man, he sure could shoot, just like Larry and Dean had said.

Chucky looked around, nobody to be seen. He ran back to the Accord, not bothering to hide the rifle. He threw it into the locker then grabbed the plastic tarp, rolled the barber onto it and, using his handkerchief, tugged the man's wallet out of his back pocket. Chucky was after the bills but he must have been nervous because the plastic and bits of paper spilled out of the wallet. The guy had a Bank of Montreal debit card and another from the Royal, and the PIN numbers were conveniently written on a piece of lined paper from a pocket notebook.

He wrapped the tarp around the barber and after five minutes of effort managed to lift the man and get him inside. Then, after catching his breath, Chucky locked up and closed the trunk of the Accord. He used the hose on the wall at the end of the lockers to wash the blood and bits of skull, skin and brain away, watched it vanish down the drain.

Then Chucky got into the barber's car and drove to Burrard Street, used the barber's Montreal card at a bank machine to draw out five hundred dollars; got another five hundred from the guy's other card. He turned onto Fourth Avenue and headed east. Forty-five minutes later, he crossed the border at Aldergrove. Chucky laughed to himself. It seemed like he was actually getting away with it. There was still about an hour and a half before they were even supposed to meet the women at the pub on Granville Island. What were the cops doing? Here he was driving south in the US of A—a free man. He could do anything he wanted. "Florida," Chucky said out loud, "I think I'll go to Florida. Too bad about the barber's sister-in-law though. But, hell, there'll be others."

PLENTY OF KETCHUP

"So, Donny, you're clear on what the man looks like, right?"

"Yeah, Sal. How many times I have to tell you? I know what he looks like and you're here to, uh, what you call it, verify it's the man. So don't bust my balls, all right?"

"The reason, Donny, you just illustrated it."

"Fuck you mean, illustrated?"

"You flying off the handle's what I mean. One simple question, I asked you."

"A question you ain't stopped asking since you picked me up."

"Donny, you're a—I'll tell you straight out—you're a hothead."

"Why you bustin my balls?"

"I'll tell you something. I'm not the only one thinks this. High up thinks it too."

"I don't believe it."

"You better believe it."

"You ain't my wife, Sal. Don't nag me."

"Let me start over here. I just want to be sure. Just think there was a mix-up."

"A mix-up? Mother-fuck, that would be disastrous. We'd have to move to like Bolivia or someplace."

"Bolivia, I don't know, Donny. You're dark enough, maybe you could fit in. Not me. My people were northerners."

"Northerners? Right. A guy, his ancestors crossed the pond, he's talking about it fifty years later and all of a sudden the ancestors are northerners. Probably came from Puglia, Calabria, someplace like that, but time changes it to fucking Tuscany."

"No, Donny. It's the truth, I tell you."

"What, they're from Tuscany?"

"I don't know, from up north somewhere. Udine, around there somewhere maybe, I think."

"Udine? That's practically fucking Sweden."

"Switzerland."

"Fuck's the difference?"

"Lots of difference."

"Who gives a shit? Listen, Sal, you don't know where they're from but you want me to believe it's somewhere's in the north? Fuck's that sound? What if this was court? This is all that you got to defend yourself from the charge of being a fucking Calabrese or something."

"Yeah, well, you're not a goddamned jury."

"No, but I been up in front of a coupla them."

"Yeah, yeah. The young kid with all the experience."

"And another thing, Sal. You're no lighter skinned than me.

124

And I'm proud of my heritage. Proud of bein from Campania."

"Hey, if I was from Campania, I'd be proud of it, but I ain't, or my people ain't from there so I can't be proud of something that doesn't concern me. I tell you the time I went back there—"

"Hey! There's—"

"Hold it! That ain't him . . ."

"For a minute there, I thought . . ."

"See, that's what I mean. What I meant. You got mixed up. Mistook the guy. That guy across the street, you see him now in the nightlight from that shop there, see he's in the lightweight jacket there, grey jacket, wearing the dry cleaned jeans?"

"Yeah."

"You mistook him for our guy, so we could have messed up here."

"We could've but we didn't on account of after my initial, my first impression, I realized it wasn't him."

"But what if. . ."

"What if fuckin nothin, Sal. I know my job which is why I got the goddamned job, right?"

"Yeah, you got the fuckin job, all right."

"What's that mean?"

"Forget it."

"So I got the job."

"And I'm sittin in the seat of the van and you're in the passenger's ridin shotgun. And the reason we're in our different places is because I got many years seniority on you. In fact what you're gonna do, supposed to do in a little while, I already done many, many times."

125

"Yeah, yeah. The old veteran breaking the rookie in. Only I been around, see."

"Uh huh. But this kind of work you ain't done yet. Or, if you have, it's on your own time. But just supposin you did it, even on your own time, you'd be in deep *caca*. You know that? You can cause people problems. You're not supposed to do nothing on your own time unless it's go get the papers, some grocery shopping, maybe cheat on your wife, you're that kind. That's it. I think you know what I mean. Bolivia? You'd have to get there, first. You get there, people wear those funny English hats and smoke pipes, blankets over their shoulders. And keep going, man. Over the Andrews Mountains they got there and head south. You go to the Antarctic, you think you won't be found? One phone call, igloo down there, one of our Eskimo contacts, do the job."

"Yeah, Sal. Yeah, yeah. Hey, we're early, right? We got some time. Why'nt we go over there, down the street there other side, that coffee shop—maybe there's some nice looking stuff in there."

"I drink coffee this time of night, I never get to sleep."

"So don't drink coffee. We'll just talk to the ladies, any around."

"An'a guy comes by while we're there talking to the nice looking stuff, what then? Say, Excuse me, we got to work now. Making a spectacle of ourselves and all that. Might as well pass around pictures of ourselves. Business cards. Hey, you picture that. Us with business cards? Anyway, guy comes around flashing the tin, s'cuse me miss, you see who it was? Why, yes, it was a tall good-looking guy and another one not so good-looking, family probably comes from Campania or someplace."

"Yeah, right, tall good-looking one. Right—with the belly and is losing his hair."

"Listen, if we didn't have to be here sittin in this truck at this particular time we wouldn't be here. This is our job. Not a bad job, all things considered. You don't think the money's good? What's so hard to deal with here? We sit. We do the job."

"*I* do the job."

"You do, eh? I got my role, you got yours. I, to put it bluntly, I'm like, your keeper, see? I'm here to make absolutely fucking positively sure. We're dealing with a human being which is a creature who is unpredictable. Something goes wrong, it's my fault. Not yours."

"Only you said it was a piece of cake, the guy was so predictable."

"Yeah, yeah. But stuff happens, what makes life inner-estin'. Good stuff, bad stuff. Maybe his kid got sick, had to take him to the hospital. He can't come down here for his regular meet with his man down here, they do their business Saturday night. Twelve-thirty, half hour after midnight. Which is in about ten, eleven minutes from now. So relax until then, get out, do your part, don't let nobody see you."

"See me? Don't worry I ain't gonna let nobody see me in these clothes. 'Cept the guy."

"S'matter with your clothes? Nice Ti-Cats sweatshirt, no more'n ten years old, looks like it hasn't been washed since you got it at the giveaway at the radio station. You got those filthy jeans, embarrass a goddamn wino, wind-breaker probably was blue long ago, wino been wiping his nose on the sleeves there; and the running shoes, sweat sock toes sticking out."

127

"Yeah. That was a nice touch. Holes in the shoes. Thanks. Feel like I'm playing dressup here."

"Call you Mister Dressup. Donny Dressup. See, you got a nickname now."

"Oh, no."

"Yeah. Guy's gotta have a nickname. Funny how a guy acquires his handle right around the time he makes his bones. Weird how it always happens. Your nickname just pops up at the right time. Which proves what they say about tradition."

"What's that?"

"What?"

"Tradition. What they say about it?"

"Uh, well, it's just how things happen, the way they always have. You take nicknames. How they pop up at roughly the same time for everybody. You know how Robbi Thumbs got his nickname?"

"No. His last name sound like Thumbs? Thumbelina, like that?"

"No. He's holding meat hooks this one day."

"Meat hooks?"

"Yeah. We were bringing in some dope off a tanker coming up from Brazil where for some reason they make some kind of beef people're crazy for. The dope is in the frozen carcasses. Guys hug one of these sides of beef, the back legs are frozen together, the beef's, the cow's front legs, at the—what would it be, ankles? Probably tie them together and then freeze the side of beef, right? So the guys hug the beef, shuffle over to where there're these hooks on rollers, the rollers on a track in the ceiling so that once you got them hooked you can just push the side of beef along.

Anyway, a guy has to hold the hook, hold it steady so the man hugging the beef can muscle it over just so and hit that hook. Get the frozen-together part over the hook. Anyway, Robby Thumbs—only he wasn't Robby Thumbs then—he's showing off, holding two hooks one with each hand, one on each track. Guys muscle the beef over and *wham!* Robby's got his thumbs inna way. Three hundred fifty pounds of beef smash down on his thumbs, crush them between the beef and the metal hook, which is kind of sharp. Robby lets out the cursing you'd expect, only he tries to be Macho Man. Doesn't go to the hospital or nothin. You know how he is? Kind of guy, he takes dope and pretends it don't make him high. Too tough for that. Anyhow, he doesn't go to the doctor. He's handling the beef, I don't know, gets other dirt in there later, maybe from wiping his ass. Thumbs get infected and he has to have them taken off. Robby Thumbs. Donny Dressup. Or maybe better Donny Dresses."

"Shit. Hey, what's that you're extracting from your windbreaker pocket there, in a baggy? Looks like a sandwich."

"On account of a sandwich is what it is."

"What's in the sandwich?"

"What's inside this here panini bun? That's gonna taste so good, you mean? What my old lady made? Ah, let me take the taste test, see if I can guess the ingredients she put in there . . . Umm, let's see now. Tastes like there's a little prosciutto there."

"Jesus, close your mouth when you chew, why'nt you?"

"You mean when I chew this here prosciutto in a panini bun. Little olive oil drizzled on the bun. Prosciutto with, what's that other taste, the nice cheese taste? Must be provolone. Got a little lettuce, little tomato—sun dried tomato. And another meat taste. Salami some kind. Too bad you don't have your own sandwich, delicious sandwich."

"Fuck you too. You got another one?"

"Fuck you, you got another one? Where'd you learn your manners? Say a nasty word to me and ask for one of my sandwiches in the same sentence. Hey, I'm sorry Sal, you should have said, for saying fuck you. And I'd be much obliged you let me share in your late night snack."

"Much obliged? What am I, in a cowboy movie here?"

"Yeah, you're supposed to go, 'Howdy pardner. I'd be much obliged you give me one of them four, count 'em, four sandwiches from outta your goddamned saddle bags there. Man needs some vittles 'fore he goes on the ambush trail.' "

"You're getting to be a bit of a nutbar in your old age."

"Keep talking like that and the chances of you having one of my four sandwiches, they're rapidly diminishing."

"Stop busting my balls here would ya? You think . . ."

"Here, here's a sandwich. What a nice guy I am. Also maybe you chewing you won't be saying nasty things to the guy's breaking you in, smoothing your way into a possible life of luxury that awaits possibly, you play your cards right. Take my sandwich, my wife made for me."

"Hummmh . . ."

"Your last supper you're having a prosciutto and provolone."

"Unnh. Whatta ya mean, my last supper?"

"Uh, figure of speech. Like Jesus H. Christ. Whatta ya think he had for his last supper? Prosciutto?"

"Fuck cares? Hummmh . . ."

130

"What was that you grunted? Was that a thank you? Thank you for everything? You're welcome. Hey, I like that there what you just did. Nice touch. Olive oil there, tomato juice squirting out the end of the sandwich, dribbling down on the sweatshirt. Yeah, good. Hope the guy notices it, it's kind of dark though, but maybe he will. In about thirty seconds now because here he comes, other side of the street, 12:31, right on time."

"Shit."

"Swallow. Don't choke. Wouldn't be good, you choked. Blew the job."

"Yeah, yeah."

"Now you're gonna go out the back door there. Put the goddamned sandwich down, I'm done fucking around here. I'm gonna drive down the street, drive by the man, check out the scene, and if there's anything wrong, I'll flash you a sign when I'm past him."

"What can be wrong?"

"Don't worry what can be fucking wrong. Could be somebody dressed as him. Maybe a tall jasper, getting her jollies dressed as a guy and by coincidence she looks like our man. Yours is not to fucking reason why, yours is to get out the back door of the fucking van and do the job. Do the man."

"All right, already. So what's the last-minute instructions?"

"Last-minute instructions is to make it messy."

"Messy?"

"Yeah. Like as in nonprofessional. No other signs, right. Leave a little ketchup around, you know what I mean. Way a berserk wino might do."

"That all?"

131

"Yeah. Make it messy."

"How come you had to wait to tell me that?"

"On account, it might freak you out or something. You'd worry about it."

"Worry about it, why?"

"Just go, Donny. Douse yourself with a bit of that blond rum. Do your thing."

Donny Dressup got out, walked south while Sal drove the van north to check the street. Donny let the guy take ten steps then started across the street, staggering but not overdoing it. Keeping an eye on the guy, eye on the van. Sal making a right hand turn, pulling over, killing the lights. The guy still half a block away, wearing a jogging outfit for chrissakes. His runners gleaming white in the moonlight. Donny starting to sing, about to go into some Dean Martin, maybe "That's Amore." But thinking better of it. Might alert the man. Instead changing to that Elvis song, one Carmen liked, the one about the Lord giving the guy a mountain. Trying to sound like Elvis. Resting against a car. Pretending to take a pull from the bottle. The man close now. Donny raising the bottle to him. The guy looking at him like he was scum. Donny thinking last thing the guy sees is a goddamned wino singing Elvis. Donny putting the bottle in the bag in one pocket of his windbreaker and reaching in the pocket on the other side feeling the blade. *This time, Lord, you gave me a mountain.* Donny singing, shuffling sideways near the guy, bringing the blade out fast, the guy not reacting til the blade is on its way home, right in there, high on the stomach to the far side of the jacket zipper. The man's hands going up too far. Donny pulling the blade out and shoving it in again. Guy's eyes on him, not angry, just like he's filled with immense curiosity. What's happening? Is this happening? Wino stabbing me in the middle of the street, middle of my life? Why? The guy thinking. Then Donny, sinking the blade again and bringing it up, feeling the flesh slicing, blade hitting something inside, some organ. Blood gushing out, blood all over the fucking place. Donny hit with a splash of it. The guy down, writhing around, but not too much. Donny putting his filthy running shoe at the back of the guy's neck, reaching under with the blade, cutting his throat. Guy making Huhh Huhh sounds, but watery. Glug, glug. Right away the blood on the pavement. Donny watching the guy, bending over to wipe the blade on his nylon jacket. Straightening up, wondering if the man was dead yet. Thinking of asking. You dead yet? Man saying: Not yet. Just a minute now and you can go back, finish your sandwich. Donny laughing at that. Laughing to himself there on the street looking at the man who had to be dead by now.

Donny figured he could start for the van but there was Sal walking toward him. Sal hadn't told him he was going to get out of the van.

"You did good, Donny."

"Un huh. What're you doing?"

"I got to get something from him."

"Why'sat?"

"My orders."

"What's he carrying that for? Fucking Magnum. He coulda got a hunchback carrying that."

"You want it, Donny?"

"Sure, Sal."

"Okay, for you."

Sal raised the gun.

"Hey . . . Sal."

And Sal fired. Donny's chest exploded as he was knocked backwards and to the ground.

Sal dropped the gun near the other guy's arm that was flung out across the pavement. Yeah, it was messy, all right. Blood every fuckin where. Sal didn't dislike Donny. Didn't like him either, always bragging. A wise-ass. Sal had his orders, that's all. If Donny wasn't a hothead, he'd be back in the van eating his sandwich. Sal's sandwich. Instead of lying there, half his insides spilling out onto the goddamn pavement.

Sal went back to the van, got in, and drove home.

ALL HE EVER
WANTED

Frank was in Tugboat Annie's, up at the bar, sipping a double vodka on the rocks and minding his own business. The owner, Annie Roma, is a small mountain of a woman who used to be Annie Romano and also used to be a tugboat captain right there beyond the porthole windows, down the slope, along the arm of the river and out on the Sound. She made plenty of money and was able to keep most of it despite a husband who had a snort of cocaine the one time and never got over it. After the divorce, Annie decided to give women a go and never went back. The woman she lives with is also her partner in the tavern on the river.

There are no televisions in Annie's place, no video games, no gambling machines; it's a place for grownups who don't mind talking to one another or not talking to one another. You want to sit at the bar and stare into the mirror on the other side of the skyline of bottles, you're entitled.

Anyone bothers you or looks like they have it in mind to bother you, Annie is there to convince him or her it is not a good idea. If she doesn't convince them, Nadine will. Nadine's not the girlfriend but the bouncer, a *large* mountain of a woman. Hell, to a miscreant, Nadine coming toward him, she probably looks like a whole mountain range. The girlfriend's a little slip of a thing.

Anyway, a minute or two after the guy came in and started talking to him, or at him, Frank looked down toward the end of the bar where Annie was polishing glasses. She raised an eyebrow and Frank shook his head ever so slightly. Then he checked out his expression in the mirror. Wondering if he looked that much like he wanted to rip the guy apart. The woman is uncanny. She's like that toward all her regulars, sort of a tough-as-nails mother hen. Lately, since Frank's good fortune, she's been even more attentive to his well-being.

The guy stood at the bar, next to Frank's chair, introduced himself. Told Frank he recognized him from his picture in the papers. "We've seen a lot of you lately," he said.

"Yeah."

His last name, one of those Romanian ones that ends in "scu," didn't mean anything to Frank, but as soon as he said his first name, "Andrei," the way he pronounced it, Frank knew who he was.

In his head, Frank heard her saying it. The way she lingered over it, proud that her new man's name sounded so sophisticated and continental, the emphasis on the second syllable. He remembered her saying it for the first time and telling him, "I realized I have to make some decisions in my life. We're not going anywhere in our relationship."

136

"Where do you want to go, expect to go?"

"I want to go to a future. Like other people."

"Don't we have a good time?"

"Yes, that's what we have, a good time."

"Good sex life."

She did something with one corner of her mouth and said, "There's more to life. I want more."

"Like what? A family?"

"Not really. Just a commitment."

"But . . ."

She cut him off.

"Anyway, I have someone else now."

And then she said it: "His name is Andrei."

An-DREY.

She looked haughty. He'd never seen her look haughty before. Haughty and, Frank had to admit, beautiful. Even more beautiful than usual.

This Andrei was "wealthy"—not rich, but wealthy. Had an interesting European background.

"Do you love him?"

She didn't like the question. Gave him a look.

"Well, I'm surprised," Frank said.

"You're surprised because I found somebody to replace you? That's pretty egotistical."

"No, I'm surprised that you're settling for something, for somebody."

For a moment, just a moment, she looked afraid.

"Remember?" he said, " 'Love is all?' "

For a moment, just a moment, Frank thought she was going to break down, but he continued, "I once heard this woman, a beautiful woman, wonder out loud how people

137

could be content to settle for anything less than a grand passion."

"That woman was younger."

He nodded.

"There are other things. He's handsome, wealthy, wants a family. Anyway, it's not like the sex is bad or anything."

"I see."

The day they had that talk was the last time Frank had seen her. Five years ago.

"Of course, I'd heard about you," Andrei was saying. "Since I met her. Hey, I know the two of you were involved pretty seriously. No hard feelings, eh?"

"That was a long time ago," Frank said. "Of course, no hard feelings."

Saying that but thinking how presumptuous it was of the man, his arrogant expression, that of the victor.

"Here, look at this. Here's a picture of her." He reached for his wallet, adding, "And, uh"—letting Frank understand how considerate he was being about his feelings—"our two children."

He handed Frank the photograph. An infant and a girl about three who had this guy's black hair. And her. In a pair of pleated shorts. A blouse. Several bracelets on the wrist that he could see. The three of them on a sloping lawn, the corner of a white frame house visible at the top of the picture, a sliver of water on the right.

"That's taken at the cabin. This past summer. You can see she's gotten heavier."

No, he couldn't really see that. And why would he say it?

"Well, you must be a happy man."

138

He sort of grunted as he put the picture away. Frank thought of her on the lawn, no kids in the picture, nobody there to take one. Him there with her, lying back on the grass. He remembered a Sunday afternoon in Stanley Park, picnic basket, couple of bottles of wine, as if there weren't another soul in the park on a warm summer's day, nobody at all.

"Married life isn't for everyone," he said. "I'm sure you know exactly what I mean. You've never been married, have you?"

Frank didn't say anything.

"Your life is sort of a part of the public record now. You have no secrets."

He wondered about that. About what, or how much, the guy knew.

He asked about the two movies they had made from the books and the one that was in the works now.

"So, you've got it made. You sold the books to the movies and they let you have a part in each one, eh?"

"Uh huh. They let me have the parts."

"I saw the one about the detective. We both went to see it. Hired a babysitter, for once. We don't go out much. Not together."

He smirked. "I have my own world."

"Does she go out much?"

"Hardly ever. She's really not the same gal as when I married her."

Frank hated that, him calling her a "gal."

"Anyway, we saw the Princess-something one. You were the guy in the trenchcoat, asked the star for a light but that was an excuse to get a message to him."

"That was another film."

"Right. Anyway, I teased her before we went. 'Are you sure you don't mind going to see this film?' I said."

Then he laughed.

"And I teased her again after the movie. 'Gee, honey, you're not still carrying a torch, are you?' "

Frank ordered another one, didn't ask him if he wanted anything.

"So anyway," Andrei said. "I read in the Saturday paper that in this new one, they're going to shoot scenes in a high-class brothel. They ran photos of some of the girls who're going to be in it. Some hot babes."

"Yeah?"

"Well, I was wondering if maybe you might let me come around to the set, check out the action. Maybe, you know, fix me up with one of the girls. Maybe we could take a couple or four out on my boat."

"What about your wife?"

"Like I said, we pretty much lead separate lives. She's become a homebody. Tell you the truth, to call her a stick-in-the-mud would be more like it."

"Maybe she's unhappy."

The smile wasn't so quick to come this time, but it arrived. Very practised. He had big white teeth, a very manly skein of whiskers.

"Hey, if I wasn't getting a little on the side, the marriage probably would have ended by now. You know how it is, a guy like you. Man isn't made to be monogamous."

"Yes, I know how it is."

Frank thinking, How the fuck do you know what kind of guy I am?

ALL HE EVER WANTED

He thought of her at their home while the guy was playing around. Taking *Playboy* hotties out on his boat. Thought of her sitting up in bed reading a book. Did she still read books? Putting it down to check on the baby. Her wearing a slip. Did she still sleep in a slip? Frank wondered. *What if I had married her, would I feel the need to get something on the side?* He hadn't before.

She was all Frank had thought of back then, all he had wanted.

Annie moved down the bar, breaking into his thoughts, her saying to the guy, "You going to stand there jawing at the fellow, or what? You want something?"

"Hey, we're friends," Andrei told her.

"You are, eh?"

"Sure." He turned to me, "Right?"

"Yeah, Annie," Frank said with as little emphasis as possible, "we're real good friends."

She continued to stare the man down.

The man looked away from her, took a card from his pocket, handed it over. "Get hold of me, Frank. Use the office phone number. The office email. Don't worry, she doesn't know the password. Let me know when to visit the set."

He left. Didn't risk extending his hand.

"Don't like that prick," Annie said.

"Me neither."

"Funny, how you get a feeling right off."

"Intuition."

"He comes in again, you have my permission to belt him around a little. Don't worry about the wreckage."

"Thanks, babe. I'll remember that."

She poured him another vodka and he carried it back to the payphone near the washrooms. Frank dialed the home number. She answered on the third ring. She sounded breathy, like she had hurried from another room. The simple "hello" stabbing his heart. Frank couldn't speak.

"Hello?" she said again. "Who is this?"

"I'm sorry," Frank said. "I made a mistake."

THE LAWN PARTY

Dan Dockstetter talking on his cell: "Cynthia! So nice of you to call . . . Yes, you heard right. Things get under way at five. That's in, um, just a little over two hours. I hope you bring the candidate . . . Yes. It's just my little way of thanking everyone who's dedicated so much time and energy to the cause. You know, people from the missions and the food banks, the hospices, the treatment centres . . . No, not too many users of the facilities . . . Yeah, I know what problems that could mean. Just a few of them, carefully selected . . . No, it's strictly vegetarian . . . No, because the event is outside on the lawn, I can't really impose a ban on smoking . . . Look forward to seeing you. Ciao, bella."

She's a smart cookie, Dockstetter was thinking as he switched off. It would be advantageous for the candidate to make an appearance and good for the documentary they're making about me. Dockstetter imagining the footage, him in his element working the crowd, a man of the people, chatting with the candidate and some reformed wino, as well; not afraid to hug AIDS sufferers. Christ, maybe it's me that should be running. Imagine a

143

real leftist as premier. Maybe that deserves some power-thinking. Like it hadn't occurred to him before. No, just every day for the last year. But the idea always seemed a little vague, ungraspable. He could connect with it now. He would be a candidate with broad appeal. No one could doubt his credentials as a left-winger dedicated to human rights and a redistribution of wealth. Yet, he was well-off financially and had worked for everything he had. Well, okay, his folks had left him the house in Kerrisdale but, hell, most people his age—he'd just turned fifty—had gotten inheritances. It was he himself who used his years of contacts in what used to be called The Movement to further his business interests. And once he had resigned as head of the Enabling Coalition, there was no problem starting up as a consultant. It was a good life. Jetting around the world, doing good works. Of course, it was often boring, having to attend meetings about how much food to serve at the free Thanksgiving dinner, or where to raise money for cell phones and first aid supplies during the G8 protests. But that was certainly a small price to pay, and it was to his advantage to be seen so people didn't think he was a rich guy slumming. What he liked most was going to Ottawa or New York to give his opinions on issues like the homeless, global warming or land claims. Going first class all over the world for the Folk Festival. Amassing all those frequent flyer points so that he never had to buy a ticket when he went down to his place in Costa Rica in the winter.

Dan D. wondered what his adviser would say about him running for office. Wind-in-the-Trees would be there this evening. He'd ask him.

It was three o'clock, and the weather was perfect just like Wind-in-the-Trees had told him, weeks ago, that it would be. "No problem, man," he'd said. "I consulted with the elders."

"I hope so. What if . . . ?"

"You mean, after all this time you still don't trust the elders? They're in touch with the earth and the universe. So chill, man."

Dockstetter acted as if he'd chilled even as he worried, and the next day mailed Wind-in-the-Trees a cheque for consulting with the elders. The man was, after all, a consultant too.

During the next two hours, there was no time to think about his political future or anything else except the final preparations for the lawn party. The caterers arrived and had to set up. The gardeners were giving the flowerbeds a last minute going over, roughing up the dirt, edging with a Dutch hoe. Then the security people arrived. First, the three men and one woman from the private agency, all dressed casually, as per his instructions, but still wearing badges. They argued about that, Dockstetter insisting he didn't want anything resembling a police presence at this party. The head of the agency saying the people had to know his employees were security guards or the whole purpose would be defeated, so take it or leave it. Dan D. took it. Then there were the candidate's security people, who wanted to poke around in the flowerbeds that the little Japanese guys had just finished making look pretty.

Finally, everything was in order. Tables covered with linen on the green, green grass. No common provisions either, but tofu done twenty different ways, noodles,

145

entomadas, vegetarian stews, a veritable mushroom medley, truffles even. One entire table devoted to desserts. Another to wines and, nearby, an antique bathtub Dan D. had found back east, that was now filled with ice and beer from local micro-breweries.

All of that arranged artfully on the green grass, the catering people standing around in their black slacks or skirts and starched white shirts or blouses. The security people in yellow sweaters. Everyone looked as if posed for a photograph.

The documentary film crew arrived, a cameraman, the female director and a young guy at whom she barked an order before saying hello to the host.

The first guests to show up were three board members, half a dozen volunteers and half a dozen consumers of services at the Downtown Eastside Care Facility. Fifteen people in all, and most of them shuffled or hobbled past Dan D. standing at the entrance to his backyard, his hand out in greeting, lurching toward the linen covered tables. Only Sylvia Cavendish, director of the facility took his proffered hand. One of the patients, consumers, residents—what they were called seemed to change every week—an old hippie named Baxter Farley saluted him with a wedge of quiche, calling, "Hey there, my man, Dan the Dude," before champing down on it.

Well, there was irony in the salute from the old burn-out, but it might make a good campaign slogan, "My man, Dan the Dude." Or just Dan D.

Next to arrive was Phil Tibbetts, a councilman who shook his host's hand in a very manly fashion, and said he was glad to be there, and he must get Dan D. aside later because the people from Greenpeace were bugging the hell out of him.

A contingent from the Detox Centre arrived with several of their success stories, recovering junkies and alcoholics.

And soon they were descending upon his backyard in waves. Some motley characters too, by the look of them. Old winos, one drunken native artist who had been quite a success twenty years ago until collectors realized they didn't have to buy a painting off a gallery wall for fifteen thousand dollars when they could wait until Arliss fell off the wagon and get it for a hundred or less.

There were schizophrenics from the hotel down on Abbott Street, some women and a couple of men from the Hookers' Rights group.

Christ, Dan D. thought, there is the raw material here for serious trouble. But fortunately, their minders were alert, sort of like blue tick hounds working the herd.

Just as he was thinking this, Cynthia appeared, leading the candidate who was followed by a couple of real cops. Immediately the film people were there to record the meeting, and a few of the consumers tore themselves away from the food and drink, and came over. He was tall and lanky, the candidate, and exuded a certain boyish charm even though his hair had gone half-grey. They had met a time or two on the rubber chicken circuit, but greeted each other like the best of old friends. In the middle of them telling each other how wonderful it was to see each other again, a pudgy man with a buzz cut and moustache, holding a plastic cup of white wine said, "What're you going to do about the harassment of gays in this city? Huh? You're going to do nothing, right? Nothing. 'Cause you're just like the rest of them."

The candidate had been surprised and only managed his own "Huh?" As well as an "Ah, uh, this is . . . "

The camera getting it. Getting Dan D., smooth, saying, "Now, this is really not the time or place. The candidate's record speaks for itself. Everyone's here to enjoy himself or herself. And Marty—" God he remembered the guy's name, it just popped out of the blue and into his mouth— "Marty, that includes you. You have to enjoy yourself at my party or my feelings will be hurt. By the way, are you still with Thomas? Yes? Is he here? It's been a year since I've seen him. Why don't you take me to meet him."

Dan D. excusing himself, the camera catching him walking away with the Gay Rights activist. People seeing it will think, Gee, this fellow Dockstetter, he sure doesn't kowtow to important people.

And people will also see the candidate standing there awkwardly, ineffectually, protected by burly bodyguards.

As he walked off, Dan D. caught the eye of Wind-in-the-Trees talking with two young women over by the chanterelles. The Indian had painted his face white, then added thick black lines, one on each cheek and another on the forehead, his eyelids blackened. He winked at him and Dan D. winked back.

After Dan D. chatted a few minutes with Marty and Thomas about how the same-sex marriage bill was progressing, he excused himself in order to act like a host, and there was Wind-in-the-Trees right in front of him. It was like he just materialized between the prostitute in the short green dress and the female filmmaker in the ankle-length sari who'd just completed her own documentary on the peasant women of Costa Rica, her hollering at him:

"Dan, Canadians go to Costa Rica on vacation and own homes there and never spare a thought for the peasant women. What're you going to do about it?"

Christ, he said to himself, I hope she doesn't find out about my little villa down there in the hills fifty klicks from San Jose.

Wind-in-the-Trees saved him, grabbing his arm and steering him toward the acacias and the Japanese maple; Dan D., seeing in his peripheral vision the camera pointed at him from across the yard. Yes! Imagine that on film, him talking to a native person in paint-face. Wind saying, "You sure outdid the candidate awhile ago. Maybe you ought to think of running for office."

"Wow! I was hoping to get a chance to speak with you about just that."

The Indian nodded his head sagely, implying, but not saying: But, of course, I always know what you are thinking.

"Next election, I mean. It's too late now. This money-ass is not going to win and you will be better, um, positioned then."

"You'll help me?"

Wind smiled, lips spreading like black ink across white paper. "Of course. You will get Judge Hoffnagel to oversee Land Claims?"

"No problem," Dan smiled back.

They shook hands, brother-style.

Later, Dan D. wouldn't be able to figure out when things got out of hand. It was after eleven o'clock, after the drummers or, rather, the percussionists had gotten the crowd warmed up. It had seemed like a good idea when he was making plans. All sort of drums, all sorts of drummers. From Cuba, West Africa, Brazil, Haiti. The old female hippies were the first ones to start dancing, if you could call it dancing, moving to the wrong beat, but still they were up dancing, being joined by the old male hippies who waved handkerchiefs or scarves over their heads. Then the male and female hookers got into it, and they danced much better. More people joined in.

The drums and dancing went on past ten-thirty when Dan D. had to reluctantly, put a stop to it. There was a neighborhood bylaw. And it wouldn't do to have real cops arrive. Of course, it wasn't him who made the announcement, but one of the security people; he'd chosen the woman to do it.

The crowd didn't take it too badly. They were good people. Dan D. remembered thinking that then.

The candidate and his entourage had departed earlier and hardly anyone noticed. After the music, twenty or thirty more people left which only made the drunks more obvious. A couple of old dudes fell hard off the wagon. Dan pleaded with the Treatment Centre people to get them out of there, and they did, or so Dan thought.

He stole over to the flower beds for a moment of private time, thinking how best to get things cooled down, when he heard a voice behind the laurel hedges—a male voice saying, "Come on, I'll give you fifty extra, you let me do it without the condom."

Dan thinking, Jesus, one of the girls turning tricks in there. Once a whore always a whore or anywhere a whore. No sooner did he think it but a voice answered, "Oh, all right."

But it was a male voice. He sidled away as casually as possible once the squealing and grunting started.

No sooner had he put some space between himself and the hedge than he heard a crash and saw one of the tables collapse onto the lawn with a bag lady sprawled on top of it. She landed flat on her back, a few hundred dollars worth of mushrooms under her and on top of her, her right hand aloft, still holding the plastic glass of red wine. She lay there laughing and one of her fellow dumpster divers—a little guy with a bald dome and lank white hair hanging down the sides—jumped right on top of her, and now they were both laughing and rolling around in the mushrooms.

A moment passed while everyone just stared at them. It was like a freeze frame and the movie didn't get going until another diver dived into the scene. The balding guy who had been exploring with his chubby fingers didn't like this one bit; he was going get himself a little bit of bag lady and didn't want any competition. He punched the intruder who, in turn, called him a "dick-head mother-fucker" and hit him back. Immediately, the bald guy was screaming. The second bum was younger and bigger, and Dan D. shuddered as the guy continued to pound away on the bald guy.

"Do something!" he hollered to the closest private security guy, who went over and tried to pull the younger guy off the older one. But another street person jumped onto the guard's back.

The woman guard was on her cell phone, calling for back-up, and Dan D. looked away from her in time to see a yellow sweater emerge from around the laurel hedge.

This guard was the biggest of the bunch but he was ener-
vated from his activities in the bush, so it took both him
and the other guy to cool the scene.

Now, thought Dan, the problem was to get the irate
dumpster diver off the property and far away. At least, he
thought that was the problem, but he soon had another
one. The young man who followed the guard out of the
bushes was joined by Marty and Thomas, the six-foot-
three transvestite who needed a shave, and a few other
"queers," as they now wished to be known. Dan, having
earlier used the word "homosexuals," had been chastised,
after appropriate groans and eye-rolling. They watched
the monk-looking wino regain his composure enough to
try and remount the bag lady, and when he was on top and
had stayed on top for a few seconds, they hooted at the
couple.

"Disgusting," Marty said. "Let's get out of here."

He took Thomas' arm but Thomas shook his head,
"Let's wait and see what he's got."

On cue, the dumpster diver pulled out his pink member.

"You can't tell it from any of the other mushrooms,"
somebody said.

"Yes, you can," Marty replied. "The other mushrooms
are bigger."

"He's hung like a cigar butt," said Thomas. "A bubble-
gum-cigar butt."

The tall transvestite called to the bag lady, "He ain't
gonna do you much good with that, sweetheart."

But the bag lady grabbed at it anyway.

Dan D. couldn't figure out what to do. He had a mental
image of throwing water on them, the way some people

152

insist on doing when they see dogs locked together. Not knowing how to proceed, he turned away, spoke to a security guard, the female. "Take care of it before one of the neighbours calls the police."

She looked at him, and got on the cell phone. Who was she calling, Dan D. wondered. Was there a security guard hot line—a place you dialed when you had this particular problem? "Got a dumpster diver and a bag lady having it off in the mushrooms at a lawn party in Kerrisdale. Please advise. Over."

Then he heard a guitar being chorded and a voice begin to sing, "*There is a house . . . in New Orleans . . .*"

It was a fifty-something man with a long grey ponytail and a T-shirt with a drawing of a full-leafed marijuana plant on the front.

"*They call the Rising . . .*"

"Ah, shut the fuck up!" the transvestite hollered.

"Ah, man. Peace, man."

"I ain't no man, man."

When the old hippie started singing louder, the transvestite went over, swung her purse and whacked him over the head.

Some of the hippie's friends were there in a moment and the transvestite's pals were on the scene too, one of the hippies saying, "Peace, peace. We're all in this together."

"I certainly hope not," replied one of the queers.

When they started fighting, that's when Dan D. found an Adirondack chair and his first drink of the evening, a substantial Scotch and rocks. On the other side of the lawn from that ridiculous scuffle, another ridiculous scuffle developed as some street people decided to duke it out.

In the centre of the lawn, his lawn, on the collapsed table covered with linen, covered with mushrooms, the bag lady spat on her hands and started pulling on the old diver's thing. It must have worked because the next thing Dan D. knew, she appeared to guide him inside, and he pumped away like a piston.

While they were making a tawdry beast with two backs, a middle-aged woman with no make-up and Birkenstocks admonished them, standing over them, actually shaking her finger. Reminding Dan D. of the old-fashioned, stereotypical bluestocking librarian, or too many women on the Left.

He closed his eyes and sighed and opened them in time to see a scruffy man stuffing the pockets of his filthy wind-breaker with food. Dan D. didn't mind that; hell, the poor man might not have eaten in days, and this sure as hell beat the food bank. But, then, another scruffy man, this one in a shiny dark blue double-breasted suit coat and grey sweat pants, came up behind the other guy and began taking the food out of the man's pockets and putting it into his own pockets. When the man in the dirty windbreaker told him to stop, the man backed away. But the next time the first man put food into his pockets, the second man was there to take it out again. The first man turned around and kicked the second man in the balls, and the second man collapsed onto the grass. Now, all the guy in the double-breasted coat would have had to do, Dan D. reasoned, was stuff his own pockets with food from the table but because he did not, trouble was afoot. There was probably a political moral in that, something about capitalism maybe, but damned if Dan D. could figure out exactly what it was. And at this point he didn't give a shit.

154

At least the film crew had left before the mayhem started, and there were no press at the party. Dan gave instructions to the security people to clear everyone out. It took another hour to do this, and it didn't pass easily or quietly but finally they were all gone. Everyone but dependable old Wind-in-the-Trees, who wasn't old at all, maybe five years younger than Dan himself.

The guy just seemed so solid and reliable.

Dan got up, went over to the table with the booze and asked Wind what he could make him to drink.

"A Campari and soda, if you don't mind, pardner."

Dan D. made the drink and Wind pulled his own Adirondack chair beside his host's. They reviewed the night's events and by the time they had finished the second drink, much of it had turned from disastrous to humorous.

"But your lawn sure looks like shit, eh?" said Wind.

"Does it ever."

Dan D. thinking: Here I am sitting in my backyard with an Indian who paints his face white with black stripes and drinks Campari and soda.

"You know, when your neighbours wake up tomorrow and see the busted table and the bottles and napkins and food all over the lawn, they'll wonder what the hell happened, and from that wondering there may develop the legend of Dan D.'s wild parties. You don't want that. These things have a way of spreading. You got to start thinking now of how things will look. I can have two or three of our young men here at seven in the morning, get the place cleaned up. Pay them a dollar an hour over minimum wage."

"Yeah, okay, you're right." Dan D. surveyed the yard yet again. "Hey, what's that over there?"

"Where?"

Dan D. pointed, "To the left of the Japanese maple, between the cotoniaster and the hydrangeas. Looks like a shoe. A running shoe. Somebody went home with one shoe."

"That's more than a shoe, pardner. Let's go have a look."

The shoe was attached to a foot, the foot to a leg, the rest of the body was in the bushes.

"Somebody else must have fallen off the wagon," Dan D. said.

"I don't know," Wind muttered. He looked up from the body, looked around, across the lawn, at the neighbours' houses. No lights in any windows, just the worthless nightlights over back doors. "I think we have trouble. Give me a hand."

They pulled at the feet and the body came out of the bushes. It was the bald-domed guy with the lank white fringe of hair who had been trying to hump the bag lady on the collapsed table.

"This man's dead, Dude," Wind said.

"Oh my God. He must have had a heart attack after he rolled off the bag lady."

Wind bent down and turned the man over; the front of his shirt was soaked in blood. His eyes were staring at the black sky.

"No, sir. This honky's been stabbed."

"Oh, my God," Dan D. said again. "What am I going to do? I guess I better call the cops."

"Hold on. Think about it. Do you need the publicity? You want to run for office, this will jog alongside you.

156

Think how the media will handle it. Your opponent saying, 'If a Dockstetter lawn party becomes a tragedy, just imagine what the province will be like.' "

"Oh, geez. Well, what alternative do I have?"

Wind looked up, over toward the house.

"What do you have in that little tin place next to the potting shed?"

"Gardening things. Tools."

"Go open it for me."

"What . . . what are you going to do?"

"Just open it, pardner, we don't have much time."

Wind got out a plastic tarp, several garbage bags, a three-foot by three-foot piece of plywood, an axe and a pruning saw. He took a rain suit off a hook, rubberized canvas, and put it on. "Help me carry the stuff over."

Wind spread the tarp on top of the cotoniaster and grunted as he turned the dumpster diver on to it. When Dan D. made as if to help, Wind motioned him away.

"You don't want to touch him. In fact, maybe you ought not to even watch."

Dan D. stepped back and rubbed his hands together.

Wind-in-the-Trees put the piece of plywood under the man's head, swung the axe. It only took one swing to cut the head off; the arms and legs were more difficult, so he had to use the saw. Blood all over the dull grey rubber rain suit.

"Good thing it's not yellow," Wind said.

"Huh! Huh?" Dan D. jumped like he'd been goosed.

"Nothing, go back to worrying."

After the body was in five or six parts, Dan D. stumbled over to the flower bed and vomited onto the annuals. He wiped his mouth with his handkerchief and made his way wearily back to the Adirondack chair, sat down, then got right up, thinking it wasn't right, deserting his friend like that. So he watched and fretted as Wind stuffed the parts of the body into plastic bags, followed him as he dragged the bags over to one of the tables, put plastic cups and paper napkins in on top of the parts, sealed up the bags with the twist strips.

"Okay," Wind said, "I got to clean this rubber suit up."

" 'Okay?' What do you mean, 'okay?' You're just leaving the body there? The bags there?"

"Sure, no one's going to steal them, eh? When the young men come by tomorrow, they'll load them on the truck with the rest of the garbage and they'll take them to the dump."

Wind hosed off the suit, the pink water running across the concrete outside the potting shed, and into the grass.

He put the suit and the rest of the stuff back into the gardening shed.

"Well, I'm off," he said, extending his hand to Dan D.

"But, but, how, how am I going to sleep knowing there's a man, a man in garbage bags on my lawn?"

"It is just a body. There's no man."

Dan D.'s eyes filled with tears. Wind-in-the-Trees looked into those eyes, both his hands on Dan D.'s shoulders.

"Look, my friend. Someone killed him. He's dead, nothing can change that. What options do you have other than what we've done? You report what happened and you're finished—not only your political hopes, but your good life as well. Think the prime minister's going to have you to Sussex Drive, listen to your informed opinion? Think the

158

Lefties are going to give you more consulting contracts? It wouldn't happen. The cops would never catch whoever killed the poor fuck, anyway, and everybody would think it was you. Of course, you could sell this house and probably get by for a few years. But you'd wind up an old man down in the food bank lineup. Think about it."

Dan D. thought about it.

"How can I ever thank you?"

Wind just stared into his eyes.

"I owe you, buddy," Dan said.

"That's right, pardner. You do."

Wind walked away.

Dan D. fixed himself another drink, took it inside the house, locked up, went to bed. Of course, he told himself as he lay back, pillows propped against the headboard, the guy is absolutely right. Good thing he's my friend. I might have done something stupid without him.

A WINNER

Fenwick wasn't in the best of all possible moods when he left the condo. Shit, no. What with Natalie bickering at him and traffic lined up for the Lion's Gate Bridge. Relax a little, stop and smell—she actually said it—and it wasn't only that she said it but that she said it like no one else had ever said it. Yeah, she should talk. All Natalie did was some freelance design consulting. It was part of a game some women play. One woman hires another woman to come to the store or office to consult on the drapes or the colour of the furniture. The woman doing the hiring doesn't really need any advice, just likes to say she has a designer; the latter, Natalie, doesn't need the job, just likes to say she's a designer. And she has the nerve to tell him not only to stop and smell the fucking coffee but to say, "Hey, it's not as if you're the only one with a stressful job."

As if *her* game was a job. I mean, come on.

So the traffic for the bridge to Vancouver is lined up at both approaches. To the west up Taylor Way and to the east, practically to Deep Cove. So he storms out of the condo swinging his case, pissed off, but probably not looking it, looking like your better-than-average middle-aged go-getter, going to get it, whatever *it* was. Has on his grey wool gabardine two-button suit and the blue tie with the yellow floral horseshoes. The tie with the wild motif, letting you know he wasn't your average suit. You see him going by and you figure that case he's swinging has got to be filled with deals just waiting to be signed. He's got the cell phone attached to the handle of the case. Suit jacket tailored to accommodate the pager on his hip. When the tailor was doing it, Fenwick had a flash thought of gangsters having their jackets fixed to conceal the shoulder holster.

So just as he's going by, you, the passer-by, are thinking what a cool happening guy he is. Not too much grey in his styled hair, this important dude, your thought is punctuated by his cell phone going off. Like an exclamation point!

Fenwick grabbed it off the attaché case handle with a smooth cross-handed move, like a flashy gunfighter, pressing the right button without looking, saying, "Yes?"

The perfect thing to say. Not "Yeah"—that would be crude—or "May I help you?"—that would make him sound subservient, like a secretary. Just "Yes?"

Him putting coins into the machine, getting his ticket, proceeding down the hall to the SeaBus, moving through the crowd, trying to act like he was oblivious to them but not being. Fenwick catching one or two of them looking at him. Fenwick wondering if the man was thinking he was an important guy. Fenwick checking out the young woman checking him out. Forty-four and still having something that appeals to thirty-year-old women. Fenwick sort of wishing he could explain to her that he wouldn't normally be on the SeaBus but what with traffic the way it is, it would take him an hour to get over the bridge. Get over the bridge in his *Mercedes*. His *Mercedes 600SL*.

Even on a day of light traffic, it took him twice as long to get to his office with the car than without it. It was only a three-minute walk from the condo to the terminal on the North Van side, twelve minutes on the boat, five minutes to his Gastown office, and time is money. But how do you calculate the impression the car makes—silver grey with silver grey leather interior—when he pulled in and out of the lot, took a client to lunch, driving him or her to Kits rather than just walking to one of the nine million restaurants in Gastown.

He got another phone call on the boat trip over the inlet, was paged twice, called one of the people back and got into a heated exchange about the delivery of reports. Fenwick telling the man, "No, no. Excuse me, but the arrangement was for delivery to be made today. Ten A.M. Look at Clause Three. Ten percent penalty . . . That's not an act of God . . . Yeah, well, we all have problems . . . I'm on goddamned public transportation, but I'm going to be in my office on time so I can make my nine o'clock appointment . . . No, you too. I don't care . . . It's called *professionalism!*"—and he clicked off. Long-haired guy across the way slumped down in the plastic moulded seat eyeing him hard, didn't care for that public transportation comment, probably; worn corduroys, dirty runners, tattoo on his forearm—Fenwick should care what a loser like that thought? But Fenwick not liking that hard-eyed look, the guy just staring at him like he was beneath contempt. *Him!*

All right. Look away. Don't play his game. The fellow's got nothing else happening in his life. Just confronting people with his belligerence. Fenwick starting to punch in another number when the lady sitting beside him spoke, "Excuse me, sir. Do you have the time?"

Fenwick twisting up the side of his mouth. About to say, Christ, lady don't you see I'm punching in a number? Can't you afford your own wristwatch? Then holding back, it gave him a chance to shoot his cuff, display his Movado. Impress the old girl. Let her imagine how her life could have been had she found a man like him way back when.

The little charge he got from impressing the woman was soon offset by the rush to the doors as the boat docked. Fenwick thinking of sheep, of automatons. Him different though. He wasn't of the crowd even as it jostled him, cheap suits, workers' shirts rubbing up against his expensive wool gabardine.

The crowd thinned when many of the people turned off for the SkyTrain, therefore, Fenwick was even more pissed off when some Oriental guy cut in front of him. Fenwick had to actually stop walking, the guy almost treading on his Italian leather toes. The guy not even acknowledging him, let alone giving him even a perfunctory "'Scuse me." Fenwick wasn't racist, but some of these people. They just didn't care about anybody else. Clannish, superior-acting. Some of them were rich, filthy rich. *Noblesse oblige*, and all that. He could understand it. But these others, goddamn boat people or whatever. What right did they have acting the way they did? And the government and the people in this country just letting them get away with it, catering to them. What if he tried to emigrate to China or Malaysia, or wherever? Would the government support him until he found a job? Not bloody likely.

164

So he made the lobby: high ceilings and marble floor, kiosk in the middle of the room. The building used to be the train station. Fenwick had a notion to buy a lottery ticket, try a bit of reverse psychology. The day was rotten so far, him high-strung and irritable, maybe that was a sign. Not that he believed in that kind of thing.

There was the beep and he drew the cell. "Yes . . . Oh, it's you . . . Listen, I don't care if you're only going to be an hour and a half late. I need the package by nine A.M. That's ten minutes from now . . . What? You expect my client . . . he'll be at my office at ten, *he's* professional. You expect he'll wait there for you? . . . I don't want excuses . . . Read Clause Three. End of conversation."

Fenwick clicked off. Cursed. Gripped the case tighter and walked up to the counter. Three people before him. Christ, the clerk was an East Indian woman of some sort. He looked around the lobby while digging for coins. Kids over at the coffee shop. Two dark-skinned ones, God knows what they were. Maybe Sri Lankans. The newsstand. A mom and pop operation. Mom and pop, Chinese. Or maybe Korean, Vietnamese. Who knew? Who could tell?

The woman talking to a customer, another woman, talking to her in their native language, it sounding like *dibbadibba ungbabadiba*, words coming out of an automatic rifle, a Sten gun, like they use in those countries. Want to get rid of the prime minister or a guy in some shanty down the street?—just *dibbadibba ungbababdiba*.

Fenwick came back from where he'd been, looked up just as the woman was taking care of a customer who'd got in line after him. "Hey, just a minute. I was here first."

The woman said something to him that he didn't understand.

"I speak English," Fenwick declared.

She responded and he was halfway into his next sentence, "This is an English-speaking . . ." when he realized what she'd said: "So do I, sir."

"Yeah, well, you're supposed to wait on people in order, not wait on your friends first."

"But you didn't hear me, sir, when I asked what you wanted."

"You asked no such thing."

"But, I did sir."

"Just give me a lottery ticket."

"What kind, sir? There are many types."

"I *know* there're many types, for chrissakes. Give me a, an, uh, six-forty-nine."

"You want the extra with that, sir?"

"Of course I want the extra," Fenwick snapped.

"You needn't be so rude, sir."

"Rudeness begets rudeness." Fenwick hearing himself, how that sounded. Rudeness begets rudeness. He sounded like a pompous twit. And was almost going to be embarrassed when the woman told him that it was surely he and not she who was rude. And then he lost it. "I don't need you to tell me how I am. Who do you think you are? If you don't like it here, you can go back to Sri Lanka or wherever the hell you come from."

"Cool it, man."

Fenwick saw the man who'd been giving him the eye on the SeaBus. The guy with the long greasy hair and dirty runners.

"This is no concern of yours."

"Yeah, it is. You're giving the lady a hard time, holding up the line."

"Why don't you get a job or something instead of butting into other people's business?"

"I have a job."

Fenwick, pissed off now: "What do you do, distribute circulars?" He looked around at the five others about the kiosk, expecting someone at least to laugh or say, "Yeah."

But two were paying no attention, two others looked embarrassed and one woman was staring right at him. A nice looking woman too—not too old, maybe thirty-eight, stylishly dressed. She was probably interested in him, the way he was standing up to the greasy-haired loser.

"No, I don't distribute circulars. I work in the warehouse at Value Village."

Guy saying it in a flat tone. Kind of scary like that. But Fenwick toughed it out.

"Yes, that figures."

"Least I'm not some yuppie scum."

Fenwick tried to hold his gaze, knew he wasn't going to make it for more than a couple of seconds. So he chose *hauteur* and turned to stride away. Two strides away, cheeks burning, Fenwick looked over his shoulder, eyes lighting on the greasy-haired guy for a split second. "And fuck you!"

Another stride and he heard the East Indian woman call: "You forgot your lottery ticket, sir."

Fenwick just about came to a stop, recovered, kept walking, head held high. His face flushed when he got this picture of going back, the greaser might want to scrap. At the very least, the woman would hand the ticket over with a smug expression. He had a quick picture of doing violence on the greaser. Working in a second-hand store warehouse. The kind of job they give convicts on parole.

Out the door, left and along Water Street. Fenwick had reached the silly steam clock before he started to cool down. Blowing off steam! He almost grinned. Asking himself, what was there to get so worked up about?

He had another block to walk before reaching the office, the building with the double doors next to a trendy coffee shop, and Fenwick was fairly well chilled out by the time he got there. On impulse he went into the shop, ordered a grande European roast to go. Before putting a lid on it, Fenwick actually took a whiff of it—looking around first to see if anyone was watching. Fenwick chuckling at himself, stopping to smell the coffee.

Upstairs, reassured by his office, *his* office, the rich creamy leather chairs in the waiting room, two glass tables with magazines, black and white photography on the pale grey walls, desks, his employees, *his* employees, messages waiting, although it was only a minute before nine o'clock.

By lunchtime Fenwick was approaching the mellow point, would have been there had it not been for the matter of the late reports. It was a setback though he was well on his way, had regained his ground by noon.

He met a supplier for lunch at a place on Water Street, tables on a terrace outdoors, Martini and Rossi umbrellas, northern Italian cuisine. The supplier was just your typical middle-aged business man, a guy with average brains, average dreams and average looks. Fenwick knew he was different. Felt good knowing it, magnanimous. Basked in

168

it. Told the story of his takeover of the graphics communication company last year, knew the guy was impressed, probably fantasizing about doing something similar. But he never would. He was just average. Fenwick picked up the cheque. Pictured the supplier going back to his office thinking, That Fenwick, what a guy. A winner.

By three in the afternoon, he was humming old songs. Wished there were windows in his office instead of great double glazed plates of tinted glass. He'd open them and listen to the birds singing. But instead, Fenwick sang.

Remembered his rebellious youth. He wasn't going to "work on Maggie's farm no more." Never did. Used to drive around in his yellow Volkswagen convertible. Always a good-looking babe by his side. *You better run girl, you're much too young, girl.* They never ran from him. No way. He was a real rebel. What happened to the rest of them that claimed to be anti-establishment? By the time they realized what was happening, it was too late, the system got them. But not him. He beat it at its own game.

He was checking out the annual report, website version, when he caught himself humming "My Way."

Four-thirty. Well, he'd leave early. Thing to do, Fenwick decided, was go back to the kiosk and apologize to the East Indian woman, the Sri Lankan or whatever she was. Poor woman was still there no doubt. Had to work ten or twelve hours a day. Life was probably very difficult, must live in a room with five or six others. He guessed she was in her early thirties. Who knows though, she could be twenty-five. They age fast. Maybe he'd check her out while he was apologizing. Check her out and take her out if she looked good. Yeah, meet her after work some afternoon, wine and dine her, take her to a room at the Pacific Plaza, have a gift waiting on the bed, just a bauble, the cost inconsequential to him, but overwhelming to her. Then he'd make love to her for hours, and the next day she'd walk around as if in a dream. Fenwick would never take her out again, she'd remember the evening all her life, the one special memory, a glittering romantic moment in the long hours of her mundane life.

Well, any hopes of a scenario like that were dashed when Fenwick got to the kiosk. He saw the woman recognize him as he approached. Saw the apprehension which he soon put to rest. That was easy for him, he had the ability to put people at ease.

"I sincerely want to apologize to you for the way I behaved this morning."

He studied the woman as her expression began to relax. He observed that she was okay, but nothing special. Her eyes were too close together.

"I had no right to be so brusque with you. Of course, I was stressed to the max, but that's no excuse."

Still the thing with the eyes would have been all right but what put Fenwick off was the black fuzz that seemed to join her eyebrows to the hair on her head.

"Thank you, sir. I appreciate you coming to apologize."

She was probably hairy all over. He wished he could look over the counter and see her legs. Surely, she shaved them, but under the sleeves of her blouse maybe she had thick black hair on her arms like so many of them do. Well, for one night. No, what did it for him was the thought of all the hair she'd surely have *down there*.

So he smiled at the young woman, gave her the full megawatt closer smile.

170

"Have a good evening then."

"And you, sir."

"Oh, by the way. You wouldn't happen to still have my lottery ticket would you?"

"No, I'm afraid not. I don't know what happened to it. I put it down on the counter to deal with another customer and when I looked back it was gone. I'm sorry, sir."

"Well, no matter."

Fenwick smiled again and walked off toward the SeaBus. He hardly ever played the lottery anyway.

He put his money in the machine and got his SeaBus ticket and headed for the boat. Fenwick felt good. He had to pee, but peeing was good. He was of the crowd but different from them. He knew and they probably knew it if they noticed him and they surely did. He was singing to himself again. *To think I did all that and may I say . . .*

He went through the turnstile and headed for the Men's. Just enough time left to pee and get on the boat. He opened the door. The stall was occupied but the two urinals were free. Good, he didn't like peeing next to somebody else.

Just then the stall opened and he was confronted with the greaser guy from that morning. The guy was just as surprised as Fenwick was. Fenwick saw the tattoo on the man's forearm ripple as he zipped up his pants.

The guy's small eyes were fixed on him, seemed to be drilling him.

"Remember me? I'm the guy you told to fuck off."

"Uh," Fenwick said. "Uh."

"Why don't you tell me that now, you yuppie scum?"

"Uh, hey. Listen, this morning I was stressed. I didn't mean . . ."

171

"You didn't mean? Hey, where I've been for the last three years you say the wrong thing and you pay the consequences."

The guy reached into the right pocket of his corduroys, and it seemed to Fenwick that his arm went in practically to the elbow. It also seemed that his hand came back holding a knife. Fenwick thinking the blade wasn't very long. Then thinking that was scarier, a small blade like that. You could picture what a long blade might do.

"Uhh, listen, man."

"Don't call me 'man.' "

"Uh, look. I think you're over-reacting. I'm sorry about this morning. I apologized to the woman at the kiosk, and now, I apologize to you."

The guy smiled, then lowered the knife, reached into the breast pocket of his shirt.

"Here, I picked up your lottery ticket off the counter this morning."

Jesus, Fenwick exclaimed to himself. And took a deep breath.

"Oh, thanks. Thank you."

"Call me sir."

"Sure. Thank you, sir."

"That's better."

Fenwick stepped forward. "You had me worried there for a moment."

"Really? No need to worry, bro."

"Good."

Fenwick reached for the lottery ticket.

"Nothing at all to worry about," the guy said. "It'll be all over in a moment."

172

The blade went in just above the waistband of Fenwick's grey gabardine suit and just to the right of the pager. The last thing Fenwick felt, after the hot pain of the blade, was the guy's fist. It was as if the fist that held the knife was coming into his stomach.

Then Fenwick slid down, off the knife and onto the washroom floor.

The greasy-haired guy wiped the blade on the back of Fenwick's grey gabardine suit, put it back in the sheath strapped to his right leg, and walked out of the washroom.

He jogged a few steps but no one paid him any mind because he was just another person hurrying to board the SeaBus before it pulled away.

He was on the boat and out of there. No problem.

The next morning, he bought a *Province* and took the bus over the Lion's Gate Bridge instead of taking the boat across the inlet. There was a story about a man being found stabbed to death in the washroom at the SeaBus terminal. Maybe it was time to break parole and head east. He checked the Lottery results. He had three lousy numbers. Ten bucks. Still, he was a winner.

PLEASE, BABY

It was a violet-coloured envelope, postmarked Victoria, and the handwriting was unfamiliar. The woman began by wondering if I was surprised to get an actual letter, personal mail having become so quaint and old-fashioned. Then she wrote that she was an "old-fashioned girl."

She had read three of my books, the last being a collection of true stories. If I were really the way it seemed to her that I was, well then, I would help her out. She had "a problem." She was dying of cancer, had a year at most to live. The reality of her situation explained the "frank, no beating around the bush," quality of her letter. Her husband, evidently, wanted nothing to do with her "in the sack." But I wasn't supposed to interpret that to mean she'd had her breasts removed and was, thus, unappealing, or in *any way* unappealing. She didn't have "obnoxious ideas," or "speak in jargon, either." She was quite a "dish" and with only these few months to live she wanted to live them to the full and wanted me to help her.

I didn't phone or write. At first, I considered that it might have been a former friend in Victoria, having her little joke.

But I checked the handwriting against an old postcard from South America. Then I wondered how much of the woman's story, if any, were true.

Two weeks went by, and there was another violet envelope. "Look, time is running out. Get over here and take care of me. In case you are unclear as to what exactly needs taking care of, please see the enclosed. You can do whatever you want with it, but hopefully *with* or *to* the real thing."

She had climbed up on a photostat machine without her underwear on, and sent along a couple of views of the original.

My curiosity was piqued but not that much. I could get into enough trouble where I was without taking a ferry to more of it.

The next letter came in another two weeks. "Listen, Jimbo. Don't be a jerk. I have one less month to live and you've missed out on a month of good—dare I say, great—fucking. I wish your phone number wasn't unlisted. If you're worried about my husband, don't be. He's in Vancouver all week except for weekends. Here's a shot of my posterior."

In a week, I received a note priority post. "I don't know what I have to do to entice you over here. I've been totally sincere in everything I've said. Perhaps you think I'm some sort of skank, and worried that if you commit to meeting with me I'll turn out to be some three-hundred pound psycho filled with excuses for why I said I was gorgeous. So, if you want to see for yourself I'll be at _____ on Thursday for lunch, wearing a green dress and 'high heel shoes.' P.S. I read your story of the same name."

176

I was going to call my friend Richard Olafson to go to the restaurant and check out the scene, but I was worried he might say something. So I called another friend, a woman. I didn't mention any details, just that I had received a couple of letters from someone who liked my books, and I was curious about her.

At one-thirty, she telephoned.

"It's Sandra. Tell me, does this woman want to meet you?"

"That's what she says."

"She make any suggestions? I mean, suggest she'd be interested in something else besides a literary conversation?"

"Why do you ask?"

"Well, just one glance is all it takes to realize this is a woman with things other than literature on her mind."

"Is she, perhaps, not bad-looking?"

"She's a fucking babe, man."

"She look ill in any way?"

"I wish I could look ill like that."

"Maybe you ought to knock on wood."

Two days later there was another letter, priority post.

"I know you have to be kind of interested otherwise you wouldn't have sent the blonde to check me out. I'll only say one more thing: PLEASE, BABY."

It was that last that did it. The two words together. I don't know. Either one alone wouldn't have had done the trick. I put the car on the ferry and called her from Victoria.

There was a pause when I told her who was calling. A pause that I filled with the thought that she was going to reveal her trick. But, no. She said, "Thank God."

177

We met on Government Street near the Blue Bridge. She came walking toward me and, yes, she was a knockout. She surprised me by acting shy, or being shy. We didn't say much at first, walked along holding hands, then we stopped and looked over the rail at the water and she put an arm around me and we kissed. Younger people walking by on a summer afternoon. I wonder what they thought about us, what I would have thought, twenty years old, seeing some guy over fifty kissing a gorgeous younger woman. Or maybe you had to be over fifty to think she was young, her being all of forty years old. Still, I wondered how anyone could not find her gorgeous. Those big brown eyes and luxurious Tahitian black hair. Tall and lithe, skirt above her knees, thin legs, like the legs of models in fashion sketches. Only her breasts were out of proportion, seeming too full for her slenderness.

She pulled away from the kiss, saying, "You know what I want to do?"

"No. What?"

"I want to fling roses, fling roses riotously."

"You do, eh?"

"And if you can tell me who wrote that, you can have anything you want."

"Ernest Dowson."

"Well, you could have had anything you wanted even if you didn't know who it was."

We walked around and had something to eat, then got a couple of bottles of wine and took a room at the James Bay Inn. We didn't come down until ten at night, for a couple of beers and something to eat in the pub. We returned to the room and got back into bed and she curled

178

up against me, legs entwined in mine, and said she was going to sleep, and did so, almost immediately, with her head on my chest.

I woke in the same position, my face in her black hair. I moved her head onto the pillow and she murmured. I watched her sleep. I turned down the sheet and looked at her. There was a small square of bandage above her hip on the right side, I could see a speck of dried blood under the patch.

I kissed her stomach and she opened her big brown eyes. She looked at me and smiled.

"Good morning, sweetheart," she said.

Oh, no, I thought.

"Sweetheart?" she said again.

"Yes?"

"You're going to think I'm really foolish," she said.

"Try me."

"Not only that, you're probably going to think I'm presumptuous and preposterous, and you're going to climb out of bed and put on your clothes and get to the ferry as quick as you can."

"Uh huh."

"Jim?"

"Yes?"

"Sweetheart? You don't mind if I call you sweetheart? It's nice and old-fashioned."

"I like it."

"I . . . "

"What?"

"I can't say it."

"That's okay," I said.

179

It was Friday, the day her husband came home. We went out for breakfast and came back to the room for forty-five minutes until it was check-out time, and then we walked around town with our arms around each other and looked in shops and shop windows. I saw Richard going into the main post office with his shirttail hanging out, his tie like a skinny red leather metronome. I pointed him out and just at that moment he turned and looked right at us but didn't appear to see us, his eyes magnified behind thick glasses.

"He's eccentric," she said.

"Yes. Indeed, he is."

We said our goodbyes and I drove back to the ferry.

The next week we met in Vancouver where I'd reserved a room at the Sylvia Hotel near Stanley Park.

"Aren't you worried about running into him?" I asked her.

"You think my husband's going to be in the hotel?"

"We have to leave it sometime."

"Do we?" she teased.

We were staying two nights. Just after we got to the room, she was hanging up clothes and took a piece of paper out of a jacket. She unfolded the paper and showed it to me. I was standing at the window that looked down on the little parkette at the side of the building.

"And what's this?" I asked, taking the piece of paper.

There was an old man and an old woman sitting on a bench down there. He was fat and had an aluminum walker in front of him. She was tiny. They both looked straight ahead, just staring at some bushes across the way.

180

"It's a list of all the ways I've never done it and want to do it."

"Hmm," I said. "Looks interesting. This one, number fourteen, in the movie theatre, might be difficult. I mean logistically."

"I'll leave it up to you to find a way. I want us to do them all before I—you know. Before I die."

I looked at her looking out at the old people.

"Well, this list is a pretty tall order. You're just going to have to stay alive for a long time."

We didn't spend all our time in the room. We walked the streets and through the park, and didn't care a damn about any old husband. She wanted to browse the secondhand bookstores on Pender Street and stare at ducks and swans in Lost Lagoon; she was curious about passersby and we made up stories about them.

"That guy. Sure he looks like a bum. But he was a doctor back in Iran. A surgeon. Look at those long elegant fingers. But his English isn't good enough for him to pass the examination to get his license. So he hunts through dumpsters and studies English at night. Learns from television."

We went to hear jazz, we bought CDs. "I wish I would have learned more about music. About what's really going on. And now I'll never know."

She said that kind of thing matter-of-factly. I never knew her to be morbid, and I'd wonder about that, about how she managed not to be.

Two weeks later, she drove north to Nanaimo and I took the ferry over from Horseshoe Bay. We met in the lobby of the refurbished hotel. It was drizzling and foggy outside and you couldn't see the mountains. The harbour below

181

was busy in a northern England sort of way. She looked drawn and pale.

"You can see the difference. That's what you're thinking, right now, aren't you? Don't lie to me."

"I won't lie to you. I wouldn't say that I can see 'the difference' but you do look tired. It could be you didn't get a good night's sleep."

"I wish that was the reason."

We went walking in the rain and stopped in a bookstore. While I was browsing, she bought a book. "Here, I got this for you. I think if I could have been anyone, I would have been this woman. Tina Modotti. This is a biography of her. Maybe you could someday—someday?—maybe you could tell me about a book that was very important to you."

"I have one here."

I got a copy of Céline's *Journey to the End of Night* and gave it to her.

We drove up to Parksville and checked into a motel on the Indian River, a crazy compound with a trailer and a cabin in the middle of the horseshoe drive. The couple who ran the place looked like retired junkies who'd gotten an inheritance. They were my age and solicitous, like they knew we were involved in a desperately romantic assignation.

"Can we get you anything?" they kept asking.

"You mean dope?" I asked.

"No, man. No. That's in the past. We mean, you know, whatever you want. Towels. Robes. Call for Chinese."

"Yes," she said. "We'd love two satin robes to go with the satin sheets."

The man and woman laughed.

182

"How about dial-a-bottle? Get a twelver. Bottle of whisky. Southern Comfort."

"Whisky."

"Hey, man. It's on the house. I mean it. You get the cab. I'll spring for the bottle."

We were in the room when the lady of the motel appeared at the door with a bottle of Seagram's on a TV tray with a plastic bowl of ice. Leaving the room, she winked.

The lovemaking was different that night. Long, slow, languorous. Looking back, it's tempting to think we both knew somehow that it would be the last time, so there was no rushing and fumbling with clothes.

In the morning, while she was having a shower, I took a walk around the grounds and ran into the man.

"Have a good night?" he asked with a goofy grin.

"Yeah, we sure did."

"She's beautiful, your lady friend."

"Yes, she is that."

"But she's sick too, eh? Hey, I'm sorry, it's none of my business."

"Yeah, she is."

"Too bad, man."

He meant it, too, that strange man.

"Yeah, pal, it's too damned bad."

I had to go away. It was work. I was gone three weeks and when I returned she wasn't home. She had sent me a letter though. She was travelling through the province with her husband on a trip to visit his relatives. She'd read Céline and wanted to know what I thought of Tina Modotti.

She called when she got back: "I felt like an old singer on a farewell tour."

She told me she wasn't in very good shape and had to go into the hospital for a couple of days.

If this story were fiction, I could put a twist on the ending. For instance, it could turn out that she didn't have cancer after all, had never had cancer or even suspected she had cancer. It was just a game she'd played with me. She could write me a note, on the order of, "Hey, that was great fun but just one of those things, eh? You really fell for it, didn't you? It was pretty funny how broken-hearted you looked at one point."

Then maybe she could play the same trick on other writers or artists too. There could be novels and entire books of stories, paintings and sculptures, about her and her twisted ruse.

But this isn't a made-up story.

She came out for two days, the last two.

Only once did I get into the hospital to see her.

I barely knew the body on the bed; it was as if I recognized her the way you recognize a figure in a collage, assembling the fragments. Her black hair, the hollow of her neck, the movement of her eyes. She wanted to talk about Tina Modotti.

"She was so beautiful."

"Not as beautiful as you," I said, and meant it.

"What a story. Came to America, became an actress on the stage in San Francisco and in the movies, was the lover of Edward Weston and went to Mexico to be a revolutionary. How romantic. I wish I could have led a life like that."

"You were stronger than her. You never gave up."

"Would you do me a favour?"

"Anything."

184

"Undo your pants and let me put my hand on it. And you put your hand under the sheets, between my legs."

After a few minutes, she said, "Now that's how I wish I would go."

I received a postcard from her two weeks later. She had been dead three days when I got it. She'd given the card to her favourite nurse to mail, as I discovered when I went looking for details.

Dear Jim:

I've read the wonderful Céline . . . My favourite line 'Life is a one-way street and Death owns all the cafés' . . . It is a true if little known fact that said line was the inspiration of the Starbucks empire . . . That's it, sweetheart . . . See you later?

Several weeks after that, a package arrived from her address in Victoria. The six letters I had written her, in their envelopes, all tied together with a piece of pale blue yarn. Stuck under the piece of yarn was a piece of paper from a four-by-four inch desk pad. Folded inside the piece of paper was an obituary notice. On the piece of paper, he had written, "I believe these are yours."

He called me a "cocksucker" which I didn't take personally, though I had to marvel at how inappropriate it was.

Then he wrote: "Think you'll get a story out of it?"

HAPPY ENDINGS

The first time John Markey did it was in Acapulco. He was thinking of that right now as he walked out the back door of the Municipal Building, release papers in the inside pocket of his jacket. He could use a long hot shower but otherwise he was fine; and there was in his step more of a swagger than a swing, and he had a whole new attitude. He felt like a cool ex-con, Henri Charrière, perhaps. Markey figured that over the years he'd read dozens of prison memoirs so he had been prepared for jail. It hadn't been so bad. No one had tried to attack him in the shower. The only depressing part was the lack of reading material, that and the sounds of other men at night. He'd only been able to get hold of two books. A John D. MacDonald mystery and Larry McMurtry's *Streets of Laredo*. He'd gotten through the first one in two hours. The second one was a 750-page paperback that might have lasted most miscreants an entire two-week sentence, but John read it in two days.

Okay, it hadn't been horrible, but he didn't want to repeat the experience. On the other hand, he didn't want to stop doing what got him sent to jail in the first place. Maybe he'd have to move to another city.

At the corner, to the right, he saw a television crew as well as a couple of newspaper people whom he recognized. John crossed the street to avoid them. In the beginning, he'd gotten a kick out of the attention but soon enough grew to despise most of those people and their inane questions. He just knew if they confronted him now, they'd ask: "Do you plan to do it again?"

And he would have to lie to them, answering, "Oh, no. I've put that kind of thing behind me forever. I've learned my lesson."

He was eager to get home, have that shower and put in a solid five hours of reading. Then, when he'd had his fix, he'd hit the streets.

On the subway, John noticed a studious-looking young fellow reading Barbara Tuchman's *The Zimmerman Telegram*. He felt like talking to the young man but the explanation would be too complicated. The fellow was only twenty or thirty pages into the book, so John wouldn't get the results he wanted. A young lady carrying a paperback got on at St. George. She was tall, attractive with her red hair falling to her shoulders. John watched her eagerly, stood up and moved along the car, looking at the ads for candy bars and radio stations and the inevitable one encouraging you to do your duty and become a snoop for the TTC.

The young lady had taken the empty middle seat by the door, in the row of three that faced across the aisle. John sat opposite her and stared across the car, let his gaze fall between a dark-skinned teenaged boy and an old woman, onto the young lady's reflection in the window. Her head was bent to her book, *Cruel and Unusual* by Patricia Cornwell.

John leaned forward, said to her: "I read that one. Do you like it?"

She raised her head ever so slightly and nodded like someone who didn't want to be rude but who wanted to continue reading without being disturbed. John respected her for that. It annoyed him to see guys interrupt women who were reading, trying to pick them up with such brilliant lines as, "Good book?"

It annoyed him more when the lines worked.

But John wasn't that way, he wasn't trying to pick the woman up. He *had* read the book. He leaned over again and spoke to her. She looked at him with a horrified expression, "Oh, you awful man!" she said, and stood up and walked away.

I'm back! John congratulated himself. As good as ever.

The old lady across the aisle stared at him with an expression John translated as: You filthy pervert. The young guy, a kid just in from Scarborough, no doubt looking for rock 'n' roll and video games and downtown girls, nodded his head at John and smiled. As if they were brothers in the chase. The kid probably didn't read anything but the inserts in CD jewel boxes.

When he reached his apartment building, John was surprised to find his mailbox empty. He knocked on the superintendent's door and the toothless hag gave him a box full of mail. "What, you don't have email?" she squawked at him like a parrot. The Polish parrot was the way John thought of her. "No fax machine? People have to write you letters and I have to empty your box for which I don't get no reimbursement?"

"I'm sorry, Mrs. Sikorsky. I'll give you a book."

"So who has time to read a book? Maybe you. I have important things to do. Like gather up your mail."

"I'm sorry. I'll make it up to you."

"Yeah, so now you're a jailbird and a celebrity, you're going to bring other jailbirds and celebrities around here and stay up all hours making noise?"

"No, I'll be the same quiet and unassuming gentleman I've always been."

John kept postal relationships going with people all over the world and he also got newsletters and notices from different groups and from booksellers. For instance, there was a fellow in Dublin he'd been corresponding with for years about an obscure Irish writer named James Phelan. They'd both read everything ever published by or about James Phelan, and were always searching for esoterica. He exchanged letters with an elderly gentleman on the island of Ibiza about swashbuckling literature, with a druggist in Vancouver who shared his interest in George Borrow, and with an Auckland librarian about Sir George Grey. As well, John received bulletins or magazines from the likes of The Santos-Dumont Club, The Tonga History Group and the André Malraux Society. There was also a catalogue from a shop in Santa Barbara that specialized in books about knives.

So there was the usual mail of that sort as well as some stuff from strangers. An anarchist fanzine wanted to do a profile on him and a university radio station requested an interview. There was a letter from the library board of a town in Northern Ontario officially condemning him for his activities.

John decided he'd agree to the interview and profile, and would write a letter to the folks on the library board and warn them he was thinking about moving to their town. In fact, he'd announce his intentions during the radio interview. He could just imagine the headline in the local rag: He's Coming Here!

But he wasn't going to let fame turn his head. John took a shower and settled down in his fake leather wingback chair for a good stint of reading. Five hours like he used to put in before he got busted. For years his five-hour sessions were devoted to non-fiction. As well, at night, in bed, he'd get in an hour or so of fiction before falling asleep. But ever since returning from Acapulco, he'd been dividing his reading time equally.

Reading was his real passion and his major problem. Or, at least, others thought it was his problem. He'd loved reading ever since learning how, at age five. When he was growing up his parents would tell him to put down his book and go out and play. His friends taunted him, "Bookworm! Bookworm! Always got your nose in a book!"

Had John not done other things in life, maybe life would have gone more smoothly. If he had conformed to other people's idea of a "bookworm," he might have found some comfort in his niche. But he wasn't a recluse or some introverted goof. He was pretty good at sports and was no awkward, gawky reject, so girls didn't squinch up their faces when they saw him coming. It was just that he'd rather read than play hockey. Rather read than go out on a date. He did go out on dates though, and had a number of girlfriends but eventually they'd get angry with him for "preferring those silly old books to me."

Despite his love of books, John had never made a living from them. He might have taught literature or history or reviewed books or written articles but he wanted to keep his passion separate from the daily grind. So in university he had studied pharmacology. The way John thought of the division of vocation and passion was sort of like if he went to Tahiti or someplace in the South Seas and fell madly in love with a gorgeous *wahine*. Every day and night would be special, walking on the beach, smelling the frangipani, making frantic love under swaying palm fronds. The romance just wouldn't be the same if it were transferred to Toronto in February.

It wasn't outrageous passion that led to John marrying Rebecca when he was forty-two and she was ten years younger. Oh, he liked her well enough and she certainly seemed to care for him. Rebecca was a teaching assistant in psychology, and John figured she'd understand his reading predilection. And she had seemed to, for a while, then gradually, she began to nag at him. "Are you going to sit in that chair all day long?"

"No," he'd say. "Only until I finish reading."

"It seems like you never do anything else!"

"I went to work today."

When John graduated, he was employed by an elderly druggist. The man took a liking to him, treated him like a son. When the old man wanted to retire, he allowed John to buy the pharmacy without a down payment. Eventually, John owned the place outright, and at about the time he married Rebecca he had sold the business but continued to work part-time for the new owner.

"Don't you want something more out of life? You want to give up at your age?"

"I can't think of anything else I want out of life," John said. Well, actually, he thought, I'd like more money to buy more rare items—but he didn't say that to Rebecca.

John worked in the mornings. Usually read from two until seven. He was always willing to go out to dinner or a movie or to sit around the apartment drinking wine with Rebecca. So it wasn't as if he was a stick-in-the-mud or a failure as a breadwinner or that he neglected his social obligations. It was the simple fact that he spent so many hours reading. He realized this had been the pattern of his life but he had never harmed anyone with his reading, so why did everyone get so worked up about it?

John wasn't a showoff about his learning; in fact, he was forever reining himself in during discussions when someone made a comment that he knew to be wrong. He rarely jumped in to correct the person; that only led to bad feelings.

For years and years, he'd put up with people's reactions without becoming particularly upset or angry. Oh, every once in a while some uninformed remark would get him going, but his bad mood never lasted long. He was an easy-going guy, all things considered. But after divorcing Rebecca, after enduring years of rudeness, John Markey was just about fed up with the unjustness of it all.

So there he was that afternoon in Acapulco. The divorce had come through, and he'd gone down to relax and celebrate in his own way. In the month before catching the plane, he'd read six or seven travel books about

Mexico and a biography of Benito Juárez, the country's only Indian president. That, in addition to his other reading, which included the new two-volume biography of Lola Montez (fifteen hundred pages in all), a history of mosaic tile work, a Boer War memoir, and a survey of Tibetan art. He'd only managed to complete one novel, the latest Tom Wolfe, *A Man in Full*. John had bought it in paperback at the airport in Toronto. It was wonderful, everything a novel should be and used to be but rarely is anymore: engrossing and filled with disparate characters whose stories are connected or will be before the tale is told—although you can't imagine how in hell he's going to pull it off.

John had bought a couple of English novels at the Sanborn store on his way to the beach and settled back into the plastic lounger with a beer. He'd forgotten his annoyance of the night before. Having checked into a hotel in the old part of town, he'd discovered that the only lighting in his room was a 40-watt bulb that hung down from the ceiling by a cord. He'd asked the manager for a lamp to read by and the guy not only refused his request but looked at him like he was an outcast. The crazy *gringo* wants to read; he's in Acapulco and he wants to stay inside reading?

He got up from the lounger and went over to the bamboo and palm-thatched bar for another beer. A college-aged female was sipping a pink drink with a pale green umbrella sticking up out of it. She was tall and thin, had on a bikini top and a beach towel wrapped around her lower body. But what interested John most was the paperback book on the bar top next to her drink. It was Wolfe's, *A Man in Full*, and there was a marker in the form of a bar napkin sticking out of the paperback, almost at the three-quarters mark. John went up to the bar, standing a few feet from her, and ordered his beer. "Are you enjoying that?" he asked. "I've just finished it. I thought it was terrific."

The girl turned her head toward him, wrinkled her nose and curled her lip like she'd just smelled something inde-scribably filthy. It was as if she was insulted that this person had dared speak to the likes of her. Someone who was, like, past forty. She turned her head as if seeking help.

John got his beer and went slinking off. He felt like a dirty old man caught in the weeds with binoculars at a nude beach for college kids.

He went back to his chair and sat brooding instead of reading. He was sick and tired of it. Tired of other people making him feel bad because of his interest. He was crit-icized by non-readers and readers alike. He vowed to do something about it but he didn't know what.

The next day he realized what it was that he would do.

It was late afternoon in the same spot, and John had gone to the bar for his third beer of the afternoon. The girl was sitting in a canvas chair near the bar with *A Man in Full*. Before he could think about it, John was there by the girl's chair, leaning down and speaking to her in a soft voice, "What happens is that Conrad and Charlie Croker finally meet up when Conrad, who has fled prison after an earthquake and made it to Atlanta with the help of his old buddy from the meat packing plant . . ."—the girl staring at him with her mouth open—". . . gets a job with a home-care outfit and is sent to take care of Croker who has had a knee operation and can't get around very well. They

195

become friends, mainly because Conrad tells him about Epicetus, and to make a long story short, Charlie becomes, if you can believe this, a preacher!"

The girl continued to stare at him for at least six beats before slamming the book down. "Goddamn it!" she hollered. "You fucking dickhead!"

And John walked away laughing.

He got such satisfaction from what he'd done that he immediately started to pick on strangers. Soon he was walking up and down the golden sands of Acapulco divulging the endings of novels to perfect strangers. People who'd never done anything to him. But he never knew how people were going to react. Most of them just looked at him like they couldn't believe what he had just done. Or, as if they were too stunned to get angry. On the third day at his new avocation, John approached a good-looking fifty-year-old lady on a beach lounger who was reading a Lawrence Durrell novel called *The Dark Labyrinth*, and began to tell her what happens in the forty pages she had remaining. The lady lifted her sunglasses onto her forehead and just stared at him like the rest of them did. But when John was finished, she said, "Thanks, honey. Now I don't have to finish this piece of shit. I've had to force myself to read it but I sure as hell didn't want to. I never could understand what Henry Miller ever saw in that drip. Say, are you by yourself?"

Later that evening, in her bed on the fourteenth floor of the highrise hotel overlooking the ocean, the woman said, "John, I have to tell you, that was the greatest pickup technique I've ever come across."

His first day out of jail, John read part of a book called

King Leopold's Ghost about the establishing of Belgium's empire in Africa, before switching to a novel. After all, what could he tell a stranger reading the book? Hey, pal, Belgium got it and lost it.

Same with biographies. Some elderly party with his book on the life of Winston Churchill. Excuse me, sir, he dies in the end.

No, fiction was the only thing for what he had to do.

So, first evening out of jail, John Markey was on the streets and on the loose for real. That afternoon on the subway had just been a warm-up.

His first approach was to a woman in a Thai restaurant on the east side of Yonge Street, just south of Bloor. She was reading *McNally's Risk* by Lawrence Sanders. "I like that McNally series," John said. "He's an appealing character."

She looked up at him, not exactly encouraging, but not dismissive either.

"I have to tell you though, in this one he falls in love with Theodosia Johnson who turns out to have a past as a cocktail waitress and sometime-hooker in Detroit. And Hector isn't really her father, he's her lover. It's their friend Hagler from Fort Lauderale, who shot Shirley. The Hawkins girl killed her father and Hector killed the Hawkins girl."

The whole time John talked, the woman had been holding a fork full of noodles and ginger-chicken suspended halfway between the plate and her mouth, the book in her other hand—it would have been too much trouble trying to read while using chopsticks. She put the book and the fork down and said, "Hey. Wait a minute. Didn't I see you on TV not too long ago? Yeah, I thought they put you in jail."

197

John wound up talking to her for ten minutes. The woman said that she and her girlfriend had been discussing him, and it occurred to her that it would be funny if John ruined her reading some day. She described her friend and told John that she always took the College streetcar west-bound at 8:15 in the morning.

When he left her, John went to the doughnut shop on Charles Street but the only reader there, a down-and-out sort of guy at the counter with his coffee and crullers, was bent over something called *Shanghai Alley* that John had never heard of. He walked south on Yonge, stopping in greasy spoons and more doughnut shops, and then dove down into Eaton Centre. Two hours of it and he only had one success, a kid reading Harlan Ellison. The kid said, "Like, oh, man. Like, oh wow! Fuck, dude!"

A lady eating a hotdog in Eaton Centre, just smiled at him when he told her the ending to Minette Walter's *The Ice House*, and shook her finger, "You devil you!"

Another lady asked for his autograph.

After two frustrating hours John gave up, returned to his apartment and got into bed with Fyodor Dostoevski.

The next day John set out early, determined to make some scores. He decided to try the university area and got lucky right away. He was in the Robarts Library, just wandering around, when he came across three students sitting in the comfortable chairs and discussing "hard-boiled literature," what one smirking kid with mussed hair and three days' growth of beard called "the only accurate reflection of the alienation of post-Depression North America."

It wasn't so much what he said as how he said it that annoyed John. "What about Hemingway?" asked the one girl. The kid dismissed her with a brusque gesture of his hand.

"I don't think you can make such a generalization, Brian," said the second fellow, a blond youth with granny glasses. "After all, there are Thomas Pynchon and William Gass."

"This is better than anything those two ever wrote," said the smirking boy, holding up a copy of Raymond Chandler's *The Lady in the Lake*. "It is pure street poetry. Chandler invests the sun-drenched streets of Los Angeles with a fabulous allure."

John recognized the line.

"He gives great metaphor," the kid was saying. "And not only that, it is a brilliantly crafted mystery. I'm only part way through it but I can see what he's doing. He's setting you up to think this tough cop Degarmo killed Mildred Havilland and threw her in the lake. You'll go along thinking like that, then he'll hit you in the end with the real villain who's going to turn out to be Derace Kingsley."

"You're mostly wrong about that," John called from where he was eavesdropping at a shelf ten feet away.

"Not only that," he added, walking over. "But you stole the line about the sun-drenched streets from Ross MacDonald."

John looked at the other two. "It's a blurb on the back of all the Chandler paperbacks."

The boy and the girl looked from him to their friend, who fixed John with his meanest hard-boiled stare.

"The lady in the lake isn't Mildred Havilland but Crystal Kingsley. It wasn't Degarmo who killed her. Mildred was no dummy. She wanted something better than life with a gimpy-legged handyman she'd picked up in San Bernadino.

So she killed Crystal and dumped her in the lake. But Mildred used to hang out with Degarmo who still carried a torch. He found her and killed her. So the real beauty of the thing is that the 'red herring'—Degarmo—turns out not to be a red herring at all."

The kid started to get up from his chair. The girl said, "Brian, did you really steal that line?"

He ignored her, took two steps toward John and threw a wild punch, such a wild punch, in fact, that the momentum of it threw him off-balance and he stumbled and landed on the floor.

"That's not the way Marlowe would have done it," John said, and walked away while the kid's friends tried to help him up.

The rest of the day didn't go nearly as well. In fact, two people recognized him before he left the library, and when John started talking to a man in a restaurant on Harbord Street—he was reading *Guignol's Band* by Céline—the man, John pegged him as a professor—balding, spectacles, tweed jacket, button-down shirt—the man smiled and held up the afternoon edition of *The Star*. There was John's face, the picture had been taken three weeks ago as he was being escorted to jail, and the accompanying article was headed, "He's Back."

"The article warns readers that you're out of jail and at it again," the professor told him. "It seems that one of your victims called the police yesterday—and the newspaper. The article also advises all readers to put a plain cover over their books. Say, would you mind signing the inside cover of this? Doctor Destouche would appreciate what you're doing. Or maybe not. Right here. Put, 'I'm back.' "

200

After John signed the book, the man said, "I have an idea. Why don't you come and lecture to my class? I can offer you an honorarium."

"I read for pleasure, not for profit."

"All right. So lecture for free."

John said he'd think about it and the guy gave him his card.

John walked home, depressed. He made a desultory attempt on a woman sitting on a bench on Spadina Avenue waiting for the bus and reading Isabel Allende's *The House of the Spirits*. She said, "Oh, you're John Markey, aren't you?"

Back home, he found he had seven letters from strangers and eleven phone messages.

It was time to get out of town.

John called the druggist in Vancouver who was a fan of George Borrow, and the man offered him a part-time job. He made all his other arrangements and four days later he got off a plane in Vancouver.

He took the airport bus into town, stowed his bags and went for a walk. There was an hour before the druggist was to pick him up and take him to lunch. Walking along Seymour Street, John saw a bar on the second-floor of a shop at the corner of Dunsmuir. He liked the name of the place and went up for a drink. It was called the Railway Club. He got a beer at the bar and took it to a corner near where a round-faced man was sitting with a couple of drafts and reading a thick book. The guy had on a Greek fisherman's cap, a black turtleneck sweater and a black overcoat. He wore glasses with thick lenses and there was a briefcase on the chair beside him.

TIGHT LIKE THAT

"What are you reading?"

"Larry McMurtry," the man said, fixing him with owl eyes. "The Streets of Laredo."

"Like it?"

"It's fantastic. You read it?"

"Yes, I have."

"Then you know that it's the first of a trilogy but actually it's the last in terms of chronology," the man said. "I've read them in order and I've got 150 pages to go on this one."

John nodded his head, took a deep breath, "Well, you'll never believe it but the hero of the book turns out to be Pea Eye. Captain Call kills Mok Mok but Joey Garza shoots Captain Call three times. He has to have his leg amputated. It is Lorena who cuts off his leg. Pea is the one who kills Joey Garza."

"Son-of-a-bitch!"

John took a last drink of beer while the man stared at him with a stunned expression, wondering how to react.

"May all your endings be happy," John said to him, and then he got out of there.

JIM CHRISTY is a writer, artist and tireless traveller. The author of twenty books, including poetry, short stories, novels, travel and biography, Christy has been praised by writers as diverse as Charles Bukowski and Sparkle Hayter. His travels have taken him from the Yukon to the Amazon, Greenland to Cambodia. He has covered wars and exhibited his art internationally. Raised in the slums of Philadelphia, he moved to Toronto when he was twenty-three years old and became a Canadian citizen at the first opportunity. He currently makes his home on B.C.'s Sunshine Coast.